Just a taste? He wanted a feast. Wanted to move his hands over her curves. Wanted to taste every inch of her.

As suddenly as she'd started the kiss, she pulled away. And he let her go, watching her. Her eyes were wide, her lips swollen, cheeks flushed, her breasts rising and falling harshly with each breath. She pushed a hand through her thoroughly mussed hair.

"I had to…I had to see," she said, her voice shaky.

"You had to see?" he asked, his own voice roughened by arousal.

"I thought it couldn't possibly be as good as I imagined. It never is, you know."

"And?"

"I can't," she said simply. "It's unprofessional."

"We passed unprofessional a while ago, I think."

"Yes, okay, we did. But continuing would be…more unprofessional."

But Aleksei's kiss had sent a current through her body that had immobilized her with its strength. Had melted her with its heat. She'd meant to close the door on it. Had meant to remind her body that all that physical stuff wasn't everything it was made out to be.

Except, it had been more. More than she'd imagined and more than it had ever been for her.

All about the author…
Maisey Yates

MAISEY YATES knew she wanted to be a writer even before she knew what it was she wanted to write.

At her very first job she was fortunate enough to meet her very own tall, dark and handsome hero, who happened to be her boss, and promptly married him and started a family. It wasn't until she was pregnant with her second child that she found her very first Harlequin Presents® book in a local thrift store—by the time she'd reached the happily ever after, she had fallen in love. She devoured as many as she could get her hands on after that, and she knew that these were the books she wanted to write!

She started submitting, and nearly two years later, while pregnant with her third child, she received The Call from her editor. At the age of twenty-three, she sold her first manuscript to the Harlequin Presents line, and she was very glad that the good news didn't send her into labor!

She still can't quite believe she's blessed enough to see her name on, not just any book, but on her favorite books.

Maisey lives with her supportive, handsome, wonderful, diaper-changing husband and three small children, across the street from her parents and the home she grew up in, in the wilds of southern Oregon. She enjoys the contrast of living in a place where you might wake up to find a bear on your back porch, then walk into the home office to write stories that take place in exotic, urban locales.

Other titles by Maisey Yates available in ebook:

Harlequin Presents®

2985—AN ACCIDENTAL BIRTHRIGHT
3016—MARRIAGE MADE ON PAPER*

*21st Century Bosses

Maisey Yates

THE PETROV PROPOSAL

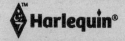

TORONTO NEW YORK LONDON
AMSTERDAM PARIS SYDNEY HAMBURG
STOCKHOLM ATHENS TOKYO MILAN MADRID
PRAGUE WARSAW BUDAPEST AUCKLAND

Recycling programs
for this product may
not exist in your area.

ISBN-13: 978-0-373-13052-8

THE PETROV PROPOSAL

First North American Publication 2012

www.Harlequin.com

Printed in U.S.A.

THE PETROV PROPOSAL

For the Sassy Sisters, Aideen, Barbara, Jackie, Jane, Jilly and Robyn. You've been there for every neurotic moment, and every triumph. You really are my sisters.

CHAPTER ONE

His voice always made goosebumps break out on her arms. Madeline would have thought that after a full year of working for Aleksei Petrov, the startling effect of his rich, slightly accented voice would have faded.

Nope.

"Ms. Forrester," he said, his voice coming in loud and clear through her cellphone, making her stomach tighten, "I trust you have everything prepared for tonight."

Maddy surveyed the ballroom from her place on the entryway steps. "Everything is right on schedule. Tables set, decorations done, guest list confirmed."

"I had to check. Especially after the incident at the White Diamonds exhibition."

Madeline bristled, but kept her voice calm. An advantage, one of many, to having a boss she never saw face to face. As long as she kept her voice steady, he would have no idea of her true feelings. He couldn't read any tension in her face or body. Or see her roll her eyes.

She clenched her fists and allowed her fingernails to dig into her palms. "That was hardly what I would classify as an incident. We had partycrashers, and they took dinners not designated for them. But we solved it. A couple of people went dinnerless for about twenty minutes, but no one was gravely inconvenienced." She hadn't realized he'd heard about that.

This was the first major event she'd coordinated for Petrova, the first event she'd done since her move to Europe. Aleksei had never attended any of the small exhibitions she'd put on in North America. He conducted all of his business from his offices in Moscow and, more rarely, Milan, saving his brilliant presence for the more essential events—which this most certainly was.

And his presence was going to make the event a madhouse. Attempted crashers—both civilian and press alike—were going to be a huge issue. Aleksei was a brilliant businessman, a man who had brought himself, and his company, from obscurity to be the creator and owner of the design house that produced the most coveted designer jewelry in the world.

His success, coupled with the fact that he wasn't the type of man to court media attention, only made him more of a fascination to the public and the press.

This would also be her first time meeting her boss face to face. She didn't know why, but the thought of it made her stomach tight.

"Those who had to wait for their dinner beg to differ," he said dryly.

She looked down at her fingernails and noticed a chip in her polish. That would have to be fixed before the party. "The issue was with the security, not with my planning. And the security does not fall under my jurisdiction."

His deep chuckle reverberated through the phone. Through her. "Your ruthlessness is always inspiring."

Ruthlessness? Yeah, okay, maybe she had become a bit ruthless. Although she'd been kidding. Kind of. But she loved her job, she needed her job, and Aleksei expected perfection. And she always achieved perfection, which meant she wasn't taking the fall for someone else's mistake.

She hadn't recently achieved a promotion within Petrova Gems by taking the fall for other people's errors either.

"Well, I've spoken to Jacob about the measures in place for tonight, and I don't think we'll be having any more issues."

"Good to know."

"You were trying to rile me up, weren't you?" she asked, annoyance and adrenaline spiking in her system.

She was able to hold her cool with everyone, always. But Aleksei Petrov and his sinfully sexy voice rattled her more than anything else in her life. There was just something about him…another reason to be glad they had a remote working relationship.

"Maybe. I would have fired you right away if I thought you were incompetent, Madeline, and I certainly wouldn't have promoted you," he said, the sound of her name on his lips making her arms prickle.

"Then I'll take my current employment status as a compliment," she said, working to put her cool, calm and collected self back together.

It had been so long since she'd allowed a man to become a distraction, so long since she'd allowed anything to be a distraction. When she'd taken control of her own life she'd done it in a big way. She'd moved on, moved up, and had never looked back at the insecure, vulnerable girl she'd been five years ago. She wasn't about to let Aleksei, or his voice, shake any of that.

"But everything is right on track for tonight," she said, her voice still steady. She was anxious to get the conversation back on the topic it should be on. Back in the safe zone.

"That's good to know."

She wasn't just hearing his voice through the phone anymore. It was deeper, richer, filling the empty ballroom and making her feel warm and flushed all over.

The back of her neck prickled.

She turned and found herself at eye-level with a broad, masculine chest. It was covered, quite decently in fact, by a perfectly fitted buttoned-up shirt. But not even that concealed the perfect, hard muscles that lay beneath.

She swallowed hard, her throat suddenly dry, tight. Her hands felt shaky. Because it was her sexy-voiced boss, in the flesh. And he was even better looking than she could have possibly anticipated.

She'd hoped that the pictures she'd seen of him had just caught him at good angles, that he wasn't really as handsome as he seemed like he might be. But pictures didn't do him justice. He was so big, broad and tall, well over six feet. And his face was arresting. Dark, well-shaped brows, an angular jaw. His eyes were deep brown, captivating but completely unreadable. Hard. Everything about him was completely uncompromising.

Except for his lips. His lips looked like they might soften to kiss a woman. She found herself licking her own lips in response to that thought. And then she realized she was standing there, staring like an idiot at her boss. The man who signed her paychecks.

Oh, perfect.

"Mr. Petrov," she said. Then she realized she was still holding her phone to her ear and quickly dropped her hand to her side. "I…"

"Ms. Forrester." Aleksei extended his hand. She was extremely grateful for the reminder of what normal human behavior was in this situation, because all thoughts had been momentarily knocked from her head.

She lifted her hand and clasped his. His handshake was firm, masculine. His skin hot against hers. She released her hold on him, trying to look calm. Unaffected. She flexed her fingers, trying to make the impression of his touch go away.

She looked over her shoulder, away from him, at the ballroom, which was decorated beautifully, everything in place except for the jewels, which wouldn't be put in their display cases until just before the event started. Until the armed guards arrived.

"I hope everything is to your satisfaction," she said, knowing that it had to be. She didn't do half-measures. If it wasn't perfect, there was simply no point.

"It will do," he said.

She turned to face him. "I hope it will more than do," she said tightly.

"It will do." A slight smile curved his lips and she found herself warring with the desire to keep staring at his fascinating mouth, and the desire to turn and stalk out of the room.

She fought desperately to gain a grip on her control. If he hadn't surprised her, it wouldn't have been an issue. If she had known that he was going to walk in the room when he had, if he hadn't sneaked up on her like that, and if he didn't look like some bronzed Adonis, she would be fine.

Just remember the last time you let your body do the thinking.

That brought her back firmly on solid ground.

"I'm glad you approve," she said, wishing that she had the buffer of the phone again so he couldn't see the annoyance she knew she was clearly telegraphing. And because it was just easier when she couldn't see him.

Aleksei walked down the stairs and into the main area of the ballroom. She waited while he examined the table settings and the glittering white lanterns that were suspended from the ceiling.

"You work hard for me," he said finally.

A rush of gratification flooded her. "Yes. I do."

"I've always wondered why you decided to work for a living. Your family is affluent enough to have supported you."

Of course he knew about her family. They were all so successful in their own right. But her parents hadn't even spoken to her in at least ten years. They hadn't offered her any support as a child. They certainly wouldn't give her any as an adult. And she would never dream of taking one penny from her brother. Gage had already done enough for her. She wasn't going to let him take care of her for the rest of her life, even though he gladly would have.

At least now he had a wife and children to distract him from worrying about her. She would always be grateful for everything he'd done for her, but every time she had a problem Gage dropped everything to make it go away, thanks to his overdeveloped sense of responsibility. She didn't like taking advantage of him in that way.

"I wouldn't get any satisfaction from life enjoying the success of others. I wanted to make my own success. Earn my own reputation."

It had become especially important after her reputation had been destroyed by a youthful indiscretion and the overzealous media. Although, even now, she wasn't angry at the press. They'd just been reporting her stupidity to a scandal-hungry public. Everything that had happened had been her own fault. She couldn't even pin it solely on her former boss, no matter how much she wanted to.

The only consolation was that the whole thing had died a pretty quick death in the papers. Another day, another scandal. But in the circles she moved in, the damage had been done.

"You've certainly done that. You've had how many people have tried to poach you from me in the past few months?"

"Eight," she said, voice crisp. "And I didn't know you knew about that."

He nodded and made his way back to the stairs. As he got closer, the tension in her stomach wound tighter, that little bit of ease she'd felt proving to be an illusion.

"I make it my business to know what is happening in my company. Especially when someone is trying to steal one of my key players."

"I turned them down," she said. "I enjoy the work that I do for Petrova." Her job enabled her to take part in both practical and creative tasks. She had a huge budget to work with, paid travel, a discount with the hottest jewelry designers in the world and, until today, had never had to deal with her boss. In the physical sense anyway.

Plus, it was high-profile. Every event she coordinated ended up with full-color spreads in some of the most popular magazines in the world. It was a dream job, no question.

But now she was tempted to take the next offer and run.

No. She was stronger than that. She wasn't going to let this…errant…*thing* hamper her success in any way. She was older now, wiser. A handsome face and flattering compliments weren't going to make her lose focus.

Of course, Aleksei wasn't handing out compliments, which helped.

Aleksei stood there for a moment, just looking at her, his dark eyes intent on her. She sucked in a breath.

"I prefer to sit near the displays," he said, gesturing to the empty row of glass cases.

"Of course," she said, making a mental note to shuffle some of the people she'd originally had at the tables near the jewelry display. She'd been planning on seating Aleksei at the front of the room. But he was the boss, and therefore not wrong.

"And that's…for you and a date?" she asked, hoping he was still bringing a date. It put up yet another barrier between them. A barrier she shouldn't even need, but apparently did.

"No, I'm attending alone. My date had to cancel a couple of weeks ago."

Oh, no. She had really, really hoped he was bringing a woman with him.

She took another deep, fortifying breath. "Not a problem."

She could be attracted to the man without acting on it. She could even be attracted to him without being bothered by it. Attraction between men and women was normal. It happened every day. Besides, there wasn't even any reason to believe that he was attracted to her. Even if he were, she wasn't going there. He was her boss.

Been there, done that, made national headlines.

"And the collection will be here?" he asked, indicating the empty display cases.

She nodded. "Yes. Once proper security is in place we'll bring the gems in."

His dark brows snapped together. "I think you should move the cases there." He indicated an expanse of open floor by the windows. She'd considered that spot. The reflection of the gems off the glass when it was dark would make a stunning effect, but for security reasons she'd decided against it.

"It isn't as secure."

"It will look better," he insisted.

She gritted her teeth. So she had to move him and the displays. Lovely. And so not easy only five hours before the big event.

She pasted a smile on her face. "I agree with you about the aesthetics, but the security team has told me it's much easier to keep track of everything if the gems aren't placed by doors or windows."

"What is the point of investing all of this money in an exhibition if the gems do not look their best?"

She fought the urge to roll her eyes. He was standing right in front of her, not talking to her on the phone, so that option was out. That meant the plastic smile had to stay in place. "As I said, for security reasons…"

He shrugged. "Then we'll double security."

"With five hours until the party?" The smile slipped.

"Are you telling me you can't do it?" He raised a dark eyebrow.

The jab hit its mark, right on target. Of course, she was certain he'd known it would. Everything in her responded to the challenge, her blood pumping faster, adrenaline spiking inside of her. Was it an outrageous request? Yes. Could she do it? Of course. And making the impossible possible, and making it seem easy, was a very large part of her job. A part she reveled in. A part that made her feel powerful, in control.

She managed to make the smile reappear. "Of course it's no problem, Mr. Petrov. I'll liaise with Jacob and see that it's done."

He cut her off. "I want this collection displayed to its best effect."

"Naturally, but I was just concerned because they're one of a kind pieces."

He laughed dryly. "I'm aware of that, Madeline, I did create them."

"I think the whole world is aware of that." Tension was making her snippy, and she needed to relax.

But this was the first collection Aleksei had designed in six years. All of the other collections that had come out of Petrova Gems in the past few years had been by his stable of very highly regarded designers. And every piece designed, or, even better, fashioned by Aleksei, went for millions of dollars at auctions.

That meant media. Lots, and lots of media.

Work was her safety, work was where she was confident, where she excelled. But this was going to be huge beyond anything she'd dealt with before. And she and the press weren't exactly on the best of terms. Well, that wasn't strictly true, she supposed they loved her. She was such a salacious headline. *She* just had a problem with *them*.

"Of course the world knows, Madeline. And that's by design. This is about business, publicity, and that means media attention. That means hype. That means big money. And that is what I'm in business for."

"You actually want the press to swarm the party?"

"Publicity," he said simply. "I would hardly go to all of this expense to put on an exhibition if I didn't plan for it to end up being talked about in any and all media outlets. It isn't as though I'm throwing a party for my own amusement."

She bit the inside of her lip and forced a smile. "Of course not, Mr. Petrov." She doubted Aleksei did anything for his own amusement.

Aleksei allowed himself another visual tour of his event coordinator. She wasn't happy with him at the moment, that much was certain, and he imagined she thought she was hiding it better than she was.

He had always enjoyed her voice when speaking to her on the phone. Low, slightly husky and always, unintentionally, sexy. Even when she was talking about the need to increase the budget for an event. But he had not imagined that the woman would match up to the voice. He hadn't thought it possible.

But she exceeded the sexiness in that smooth, sultry voice. Wavy brown hair that shimmered golden in the light as it cascaded over her shoulders, blue eyes that were enhanced by thick lashes. But it was her body that had his libido fighting to slip its leash. Politically incorrect as it might be, he found her curves captivating.

Full breasts, a slender waist, and round hips that drew his attention with their gentle sway when she walked.

She seemed to have a physical effect on him, like strong alcohol. She was intoxicating.

He put his hands in his pocket, felt his cellphone in his right one and gripped it tightly. He suddenly wished he could call Olivia, not because he missed the woman who had been his mistress until a few weeks ago, but because he longed for the distraction of her. But Olivia had been getting clingy. She had started wondering why he only saw her for special events and sex. Had started wanting him to come to Milan just to see her. That was when he'd known it was time to end things. He didn't get any sort of satisfaction out of hurting women. He made his intentions clear from the beginning.

Keeping a casual, long-term mistress was his preference. It was better than going out to bars every weekend to pick women up. After all he'd experienced in his thirty-three years, he felt far too old.

"And what do you intend to do tonight?" he asked.

He could tell she was forcing the smile that was stretched so determinedly across her face. "I intend to do what you pay me to do and coordinate the exhibition."

"I assumed you would have it coordinated at this point."

"The important things, yes. But just in case we end up short a shrimp cocktail or something I like to make sure I'm on hand to ensure there isn't anyone…" she waved a hand in the air "…*sans* shellfish."

"Fine if you need to oversee that, but I don't want you running around the party in jeans and a headset."

"I don't do that," she said.

"Good. I like for everything to blend seamlessly at these events. The only thing the guests should notice is the jewelry."

"I can assure you, Mr. Petrov, that's my aim as well."

"I would prefer if you dressed as an attendee of the party, and not as staff."

He could tell that annoyed her too. The glitter in her blue eyes was in direct contrast with the serene, smooth expression on her face. "I was planning on wearing black pants and a black top, just like the waitstaff."

"But you aren't one of the waitstaff. You work directly for Petrova Gems, and I wish your attire to reflect that."

That was how he ran things. Impeccably. In the design world, looks were truly everything. Nothing else mattered other than the external. So long as the exterior glittered, nothing else counted.

"You should take the time to enjoy the party," he said.

She pursed her pretty lips into a sour pout. "I don't mix business with pleasure."

"I don't either. I prefer my pleasure uninterrupted."

A slow flood of crimson colored her cheeks. It amazed him. He hadn't known there was still anyone in the real world who blushed over casual innuendo.

"And by enjoying the party," he continued, "I mean circulate, listen to conversation, find out what appeals to the guests, and what doesn't. Another reason to dress to blend in."

"So, I'm conducting a covert survey?"

"Not quite. But it pays to learn from critique."

A strange look passed over her face. "Media critique?"

"Sometimes."

"I don't want to say anything out of line, Mr. Petrov, but you've hired me to coordinate the event so…"

"So you want me to trust you rather than dictate?"

She nodded once, brown hair shimmering over her shoulder.

"Sorry," he said, "I did hire you to coordinate, but I'm a perfectionist, and as long as I'm here, I'll see everything done to my standards."

That did make her bristle, that fixed grin seriously faltering. "I can assure you, I do everything to your standards, whether you're here or not."

"That remains to be seen."

"Then, if you'll excuse me, I need to finish some last-minute details. Something to do with shifting seating and doubling security."

The ice in her tone, the fact that she dared to speak to him that way, amused him. He was used to a lot of sycophantic scraping and bowing. That was something he'd always appreciated about Madeline over the phone. She was direct, and she did her job. His ego didn't need another person living to fawn over him. He preferred the fact that Madeline had a mind of her own.

He stuck his hand in his pocket, his cellphone still there. He could call Olivia. Could call a host of women who had given him their numbers recently. Numbers he had kept but never dialed.

Instead he leaned against the railing of the grand marble staircase and watched Madeline clack around the spacious ballroom on her high heels.

Madeline turned and looked over her shoulder, she forced a tight smile when she saw him watching her, but he could see the tension coming off her petite frame in palpable waves.

Something he understood about Madeline: she liked control. And so did he. And he had just come into her domain, as far as she was concerned, and taken her control.

He chuckled softly and took his phone out of his pocket before he walked into the hallway. Maybe he would get a date for the evening. Madeline could add another setting as easily as she'd removed it. He could find himself a woman to keep him company tonight.

And forget about that brief flash of attraction he'd felt when he'd seen Madeline for the first time. An attraction he had no intention of acting on. He didn't date employees, and he had no plan of starting a relationship with a woman who seemed as young as Madeline did.

Because he had no intention of having a relationship at all.

He looked at his phone, then put it back in his pocket.

CHAPTER TWO

HE DIDN'T have a date. Aleksei strode down the long hallway, his blood pounding heavily in his veins. He had not called anyone. Not Olivia to see if she might want to briefly rekindle their year-long affair. Not any of the jewelry models—beautiful women—who had made passes at him over the past few months.

Because none of them had appealed. The only woman he'd been able envision had been his event coordinator. Beautiful, tightly wound Madeline with the glossy brown hair and curves that seemed to come straight out of every male fantasy.

Beautiful women were easy to come by. He had money, he had influence. If he wanted female company, he could have it.

Yet he was walking to Madeline's room. Compelled to see her again. And he was following the compulsion because, truly, the desire for anything was so foreign to him that he was honestly fascinated by it.

He knocked on the door to Madeline's suite, the one his company, he, in fact, was paying for. He always paid for his employees to stay in the best accommodations when they traveled. Mostly because he never wanted to hear anyone complaining about doing a subpar job because they'd lost sleep on a lumpy mattress.

He heard Maddy's voice coming through the thick door. "Just a second."

He could hear her palms hit the wood as she checked the peephole. When she opened the door, her expression was wary. "Mr. Petrov, is something wrong?"

"Nothing." He walked past her and into the suite.

She moved to the other side of the room, her discomfort with his presence obvious. She was so soft and petite and for a brief moment so lost-looking that he felt a twinge of something…protectiveness, maybe, in his chest.

It was only natural. She was young, maybe in her mid-twenties, and he knew the kinds of things the world had in store for the young and naive. Knew that there was pain out there so intense, that there were rock bottoms so low most people couldn't imagine them. Because he'd been there.

Her eyes clashed with his, her expression guarded for a moment. There was a wariness there, a hardness that didn't match her age. Perhaps she wasn't as naive as he'd imagined. Maybe she knew about the dark side of life already.

She was young, but there was no youthful innocence in her face. Not a trace of naiveté. She was waiting for the angle. Waiting to find out things were about to fall apart around her.

He knew that feeling well.

"I have decided that I would like a companion for the evening," he said.

She gave him a baleful look. "Which means you need me to add the setting that you just had me take away, for the date that you had, but then didn't have and forgot to tell me you no longer had."

A reluctant chuckle got caught in his throat. "Something like that. But I think you'll be able to handle things."

"Well, thanks," she said, her voice flat.

"Madeline, I was wondering if you would like to sit at my table, as a spot has just opened up."

Acid burned in Maddy's stomach. He was just going to have her be his date? Some kind of convenient replacement? It was typical. Most men didn't care who a woman was as long as she was available and willing.

She bit her lip. Hard. She was neither. And she refused to be taken advantage of ever again.

"I'm not actually interested in being your back-up," she ground out.

"That isn't what I was asking. You're an intelligent woman, Madeline. You're ambitious too. I haven't missed that in our conversations together. I thought you might appreciate the chance to sit at my table, to speak to the guests, learn more about the industry. There is room at the table, and I thought you might like the opportunity."

Okay, that was tempting. More than. The fact that she was extremely drawn to the industry of design made her job more enjoyable. She loved everything about the company, and had thoroughly enjoyed the year she'd worked for Aleksei already.

It was tempting because it might give her a chance to learn more so that she could advance into another position at Petrova. It wasn't really part of her five-year plan, but it would be pretty amazing. Something she would readily consider.

"But, as far as the other people at the table are concerned…"

"If you want to be presented as my date so that you aren't treated like the help I have no problem with that at all."

The help. Oh, yes, and people in this circle would treat her like the help if they knew she was the event coordinator. Working for a living was quite frowned upon in such levels of society.

Not that she cared, but she didn't really want to be the focus of conversation.

She bit her lower lip then released it quickly, realizing what an indecisive, nervous gesture it was. She wasn't an indecisive, nervous girl. This was a chance to further her career a little bit.

But it reminded her too much of working for William, her first boss when she'd graduated from college. Of everything that had happened. Of how incredibly, unforgivably stupid she'd been.

Her stomach knotted fiercely.

This is different.

It was different because she was different. She wasn't some naive girl desperately seeking love and affection. She was a woman. She knew her own mind, she made things happen for herself, and she would never allow herself to be a victim. Never again.

She certainly wasn't going to let past disasters stop her from succeeding.

Besides, she wasn't seducible. She wasn't suddenly going to morph into her past self. Even if Aleksei was the most gorgeous man she could remember seeing, and even if his dark eyes did promise that he might actually know what to do with a woman in bed.

She felt her skin heat and she took a deep breath to try and cool herself down. It wasn't doing her any good to think of him like that. It didn't matter how he was with women, because she would never be among their number.

Didn't want to be. No matter how sexy he was.

"I had some gems set aside for my date to wear tonight, prior to our separation. I would like you to wear them."

The very idea of it made her stomach turn slightly. She didn't like the thought of wearing jewelry meant for another woman, regardless of the fact that this wasn't a date. It was still...well, it reminded her too much of things that had gone on before in her life.

"It probably won't match my handbag. It's a really bright yellow," she said, trying to wiggle out of having to wear the jewels. "And I already have a matching necklace."

He looked at her closely, dark eyes appraising her in a way that had her feeling as though he was looking beneath her skin, into her soul. At all of her secrets.

"I have a piece that would be perfect for you."

The way he said that, *perfect for you,* it was so personal. It made her heart squeeze, and she wasn't really sure why.

"I have a very strict policy on keeping business business, as I said before," she said.

"And this is business," he said, dark eyes impassive again, when before they'd been...hot. "An extension of your job for the evening. Petrova Gems is about romance. It's about making a woman feel as though she's buying not just jewelry but a lifestyle, a fantasy. We need to present a fantasy that goes beyond location, decor and sparkling gems. It's about the woman, how she feels in the jewels, how they make other people feel about her. They are meant to be worn, not simply displayed."

She nodded slowly. "Is that in a print ad or a commercial? Because it should be," she said.

He chuckled, the sound rough, as though he wasn't accustomed to it. "If that's an endorsement, I might have to use it."

"Actually, it might be nice to have something like that written lightly, almost hidden, in script around the display cases for the next exhibition."

"I like that idea," he said, the corners of his mouth curving very slightly.

Why did it made her stomach feel warm when he smiled? It could hardly be called a smile, and she certainly shouldn't be feeling anything. It was just because he liked her idea, because tonight was looking like a serious boon for her career within Petrova Gems. Who wouldn't be happy about that?

"If you would like, I can send over a stylist to help you with your wardrobe."

She bit the inside of her cheek. She wasn't taking gifts. "I have my own dress. Thank you, though."

He moved closer to her, his dark eyes locked on hers. He smelled good. Not like cologne, but just clean. Musky and male. It made her want to draw closer to him, to breathe him in.

She hadn't realized she was verging on pathetically lonely. That was all it was, though. Loneliness. She hadn't seen her brother and his family in too long, and she didn't really have any close friends. She just wanted to be close to someone. She needed to get a cat.

"You are a stubborn woman, Madeline," he said.

"It's been said more than once," she said. "Is that a bad thing?"

"Not at all. I can appreciate the quality since it is one we share."

She felt a smile stretch across her face, without her permission. "Well, I'm glad it doesn't count against me."

He looked like he might move closer. Time stretched on slowly, the air between them thick. "Not at all," he said.

Aleksei turned and walked out of her hotel room, the door clicking shut behind him. Maddy sank onto the couch, suddenly conscious of the fact that her legs were shaking.

She had no idea what had just happened. Well, she was afraid she *did* know. She was attracted to him, to a man who was no different than any other. Discarding women at a moment's notice without any feeling or regret.

It didn't matter how attracted she was. She'd felt attracted to men, from a distance, in the past five years. She simply hadn't acted on it. Of course, she and Aleksei were in close proximity. And it was very likely they would be off and on over the course of the next few months for the different exhibitions for the new line.

She drew her knees up to her chest. Okay, so the attraction was a complication, but it wasn't anything she couldn't handle. She was an adult. She wasn't some naive innocent girl. And she was in control of the situation.

Anyway, other than that brief moment, she had no reason to believe Aleksei saw her as anything more than an efficient little worker bee. And his offer tonight had been strictly business too.

And if he could be strictly business, so could she.

Madeline examined her reflection in the mirror. She was happy with what she'd done. Very happy. Her makeup was natural, making her blue eyes look bright and exotic, and her hair had been tamed into a high, sleek ponytail that cascaded over one shoulder.

She turned slightly, and looked at her bare back, exposed by the low V of her little black dress. She'd seen the dress in a window on her first day in Milan and hadn't been able to pass it up, even though she'd had no clue where she would wear it.

She didn't normally show so much skin, but then, she was usually working when she went to parties.

Always the coordinator, never the guest.

She couldn't actually remember the last time she'd dressed up for something. She liked looking nice, but she always dressed for work, not for going out.

Something that was noticeably absent from her look were the promised jewels. She had a very uneasy feeling that they were due to arrive very soon, with the man himself.

A small shiver wound through her at the thought of Aleksei Petrov. She shook her head. She shouldn't be thinking of him as anything other than her boss. Of course, that had been much easier to do before she'd seen the man in the *über*-gorgeous flesh. Before she'd smelled that faint masculine scent that was so uniquely him.

She made an extremely childish face at her reflection and picked up the canary-yellow clutch bag that had saved her from recycled jewels from the vanity.

When she heard the firm knock on the door, she knew immediately who it was. Aleksei's knock wasn't a request, it was a demand. Like every word he spoke. And that should not, in any way, be a positive quality, and yet she couldn't help admire that in him. The confidence. The absolute surety he seemed to have that he was right.

"Come in," she said, hoping she sounded like the confident businesswoman that she was. At least, she'd been a confident businesswoman a couple of hours ago. It hardly seemed like one meeting with her gorgeous boss should change that.

The door opened and she turned, her breath catching in her throat, making a choking sound. Her face heated. Stupid that he affected her this way. Stupid that she was so obvious. Maybe she should have jumped back into dating, had some flings at least, after The William Fiasco.

Sadly, though, she hadn't. She'd lived like a nun, *sans* habit, and now all of that was starting to catch up with her.

"Does this meet with your approval?" she asked, the question tart because she was frustrated with herself for being so affected by him. And with him for being so appealing.

The slow burn of his gaze made her feel hot all the way to her toes. "It will do."

And why did that—that phrase that was designed to get her hackles up—sound like the most sinful compliment she'd ever received.

"I brought your jewels," he said, holding up a slender velvet box.

She walked to the center of the room. She knew he would follow her, but she had to try and get some distance between them. He was messing with her head, and she couldn't allow that.

"I thought you would have some of the...how did you put it?...*the help* bring my jewels."

She was treated to another slight almost-smile as he walked to where she was standing. "I send others to do my dirty work, not to do pleasant things."

He opened the box and revealed a pair of earrings with yellow pear-cut diamonds at the center and a ring of white diamonds around the outside of the center gem. The cut and clarity of the gems was flawless, the design clean, but arresting.

"These are amazing," she said, touching one of them lightly. "You really are an artist."

She looked up at Aleksei. His expression was hard like granite, dark eyes flat. "They sell well," he said.

"But there's...there's more than that to it," she said.

"No. It's business. There is nothing more to it than the bottom line."

She didn't know why, but the cold, stark sentiment seemed extremely sad, especially when it was said about something so beautiful. She loved Aleksei's pieces. There was something more to them than aesthetics alone. Or maybe there wasn't.

Looking at him now, at his unreadable expression, she wondered. The man himself was hard, ruthless. Maybe it really was all about the money. It shouldn't bother her. She shouldn't feel anything at all about her boss.

The fact that he made money was good for her. That was all that should matter.

She reached out and took the box from his hand, setting it on the vanity top, and leaned in, putting on the first earring. She raised her eyes and they caught his in the reflection of the mirror. She saw it again, that flicker of heat, and she felt it. Low in her belly, impossible to ignore.

Madeline looked back down at the jewelry box and put more focus than was strictly necessary on putting the second earring in.

"Beautiful," he said, moving nearer to her.

He was behind her, so close she could feel the heat from his body. His masculine scent, the one that had been tormenting her all day, enveloped her.

He reached up and touched one of the earrings. "There is one thing I truly love about working with jewelry," he said. "On its own, a gem is nice to look at. In a well-designed setting, cut to perfection, even more so. But when the jewelry is on a beautiful woman… that's when it truly shines."

Oh, he was good. A far too familiar feeling, an ache, a need, began to grow in her stomach. Beautiful. He'd called her beautiful. It made her want to hear more. She wanted to soak up the attention, the compliments. To feel important and…special.

No.

Madeline had indulged that hollow need before. Had allowed years of neglect to make her vulnerable to a man who talked smooth and offered her things she'd craved most in life. At least William had pretended to offer them to her.

She turned and realized her mistake too late. Her

breasts touched his chest and she gripped the edge of the vanity to keep herself steady.

She forced a smile. "That's nice. I mean, another one for the ad campaign." She slipped past him and moved further from him until she could breathe again. "We should...I should...you can do what you like, of course, but I should head down now. Just some last minute rounds."

He nodded, faint amusement evident on his face. "Of course. Let's go see if this party is as perfect as you've promised me it will be."

CHAPTER THREE

EXTRAVAGANT parties and lavish settings were, almost literally, an everyday occurrence for Maddy. But she worked behind the scenes, coordinating, planning, directing. It was her job to be invisible.

Now, suddenly, she felt quite visible.

People were staring. She knew they weren't really staring at her. It was the jewels she was wearing. It was Aleksei, walking so close to her. The man exuded dark sexuality. Danger and extreme attractiveness in a perfectly tailored tuxedo.

The women in the room were nearly falling out of their chairs to get a closer look. Although, it could have been the jewelry that held their attention so raptly. She doubted it, but it was possible.

She smiled at a passing couple and noticed that Aleksei made no indication that he'd seen them at all. His face stayed rigid, set, unmoving as they walked through the ballroom. He exuded power and charisma, but it certainly wasn't because he was making an effort.

"You might try smiling," she whispered.

He leaned down and she caught another hint of his scent. Her stomach tightened. "Why?"

She took a step to the side, putting some distance between them, as they continued walking. "It's friendly. It's what people do."

"I don't know that I would characterize myself as friendly," he said.

"But you *are* a businessman," she said, the reminder inane and pointless. She continued on anyway. "And selling yourself is a part of selling your product."

He turned to her, eyebrows raised.

"Which you know," she continued.

She didn't really like the fact that she seemed to say stupid, pointless things around the man. She did fine on the phone with him. But then, he wasn't really there when she was talking to him on the phone, and in person he was impossible to ignore.

"Whether or not I smile, the jewelry will still sell," he said blandly.

"Yes, well, I'm sure but…"

"And anyway, if you give people everything they want, they lose interest. Better to leave a little mystery."

Well, mystery he had down. His private life was extremely private. There was never even a hint of scandal, no information on the women he dated. Nothing. Which seemed sort of amazing given the media's ravenous hunger for scandal.

"If the press allows you some mystery, I suppose that's a wise choice," she said, looking away from him.

She looked around the room, and suddenly she felt claustrophobic. She was used to these events, but she was used to being on the outside of them. Being the staff meant she was able to hover around the edges. But actually being a guest, and being with Aleksei, well, that was getting her a lot of attention she'd rather not have.

Maddy had never really known what to do with a lot

of attention, having never received a lot of it. And it had only got worse after her time in the unwanted spotlight.

Somehow, it made her feel better that Aleksei seemed to feel the same way she did. She felt him go tense next to her, his hand tightening against her back as he guided her on. She looked at him and noticed a slight line of tension on his brow. His focus wasn't on her, though, but on the table they were heading toward, the table that was already half-filled with guests that were chatting and admiring the display cases filled with jewelry.

He didn't want to sit at the table. And that was when she realized something about her unyielding boss. He was as uncomfortable as she was. He hid it well, his expression almost smooth, but she could feel his discomfort.

She continued on, his hand still resting on her back, and he followed, his movements stiff now.

He did actually smile at the people who were sitting at the table as he pulled her chair out for her and motioned for her to sit down. No one else would know he wasn't completely thrilled to be in their company. He seemed as in control as ever. But she could tell. It was there, his body rigid, his jaw locked tight, even as he smiled.

When he sat next to her and placed his hand flat on the white linen tabletop, instinct took over and she rested her hand lightly over his, the gesture meant to offer comfort. A connection. It ended up being much more than that.

Lightning skittered from her palm up her arm and into her chest, jump-starting her heart and heating her from the inside out. She pulled her hand away slowly and, she hoped, casually.

She looked down at the empty plate in front of her and hoped that her heartbeat wasn't audible to everyone at the table. She didn't know why she'd done that. She wasn't a touchy-feely sort of person. Most of her life had lacked in physical human contact, and she'd never been overly affectionate as a result. She'd never really had the chance to be.

She had no idea why it had suddenly seemed the most natural thing in the world to touch him.

Aleksei could feel the heat from Madeline's touch, but even more he felt the comfort she offered in the gesture. He swallowed and tightened his fist, turning his focus on the woman that was speaking to him.

"Mr. Petrov, it's lovely to see you here."

"And so exciting to see your new collection," one of the other women purred.

He started to talk about the collection, about the pieces. But his focus was still on Madeline's unconscious touch. He gritted his teeth. It reminded him of things long past. Affectionate touches. Touches that were about more than sex. A connection that went beyond bodies.

He'd shut that part of his brain down. That part of his life was gone. Paulina was gone. Any connection he had imagined between Madeline and himself was simply that. Imagined. He didn't have it in him to give, or receive, any more than that.

Maddy folded her hands in her lap. Her palm still burned.

She watched Aleksei as he spoke. He was confident when he talked about his work, at ease with the subject.

She knew he had passion for his work. She'd seen moments of it, heard it when they'd spoken together on the phone and discussed plans for exhibitions and events. But now, there was nothing. He'd done it earlier in the hotel room. He was a master at creating and maintaining distance, at controlling his interactions with people wholly and absolutely. A skill she wished she could learn.

Sitting next to him, so close his arm kept brushing hers, proved to be disturbing on so many levels. Well, it was really just one level, but it was the one level she was trying to ignore above all others.

Every time he touched her it burned all the way from her shoulder through her body and before long she was wrecked from keeping herself from jumping out of her chair.

"I think I need some air," she said softly, when the plates had been cleared. She also needed to check on a few things and she certainly didn't want to draw attention to the fact that she was staff. It would make it interesting that she was sitting with Aleksei. And she didn't want to be interesting, didn't want to be memorable. Didn't want to be in the headlines in the morning.

Waving politely, a gesture that everyone ignored, she stood from the table and picked her way through the crowd until she'd made her way over to one of the buffet tables. Ah, low on shrimp. She'd expected that to happen.

Rather than finding a waiter to handle it, she skirted the perimeter of the room and made her way out into the long, empty corridor just outside the ballroom.

She nearly sagged with relief when she was away from the loud, frenetic atmosphere. She backed up, heels clicking on the marble floor, and leaned against the tile wall. The chill bit into her bare back. But she needed it, needed anything that could help put out the smoldering flame that Aleksei seemed to have lit inside of her.

"Are you all right?"

Out of the frying pan and right back into the fire.

She turned and saw Aleksei standing there, and suddenly the coolness from the wall wasn't helping at all.

"You don't like crowds?" he asked.

She stiffened. "You don't like parties."

He shrugged and began to walk toward her. "I would think that was obvious. If I liked them, I would attend more of them."

"But everyone wants to talk to you." The words just slipped out and she wished, she really wished, she could pretend she didn't know what had inspired them. But the lonely girl that still lived somewhere inside her would have loved to go somewhere and have everyone talk to her. Look at her. Think she was special.

She shut the door on those feelings. It was no use feeling sad about things that couldn't be changed. Wallowing in that loneliness…she knew exactly where that led to.

"Yes. Because everyone wants a piece of wealth and power. If I were one of the waiters do you supposed everyone—anyone—would want to talk to me?"

"Having spent the past few years as event staff, I can honestly tell you no. No one would talk to you."

He came to stand in front of her, looking dangerously attractive and like an invitation to every sin she was trying so hard not to commit again. "So then, why should it matter if people want to talk to me when their only concern is for my status, and what it can do for them?"

She looked down at her yellow shoes and admired the way the straps were woven together. Better than admiring her boss in a tux. "I—I suppose it doesn't matter when you put it like that."

He looked over his shoulder, back toward the ballroom door. "I simply don't have the patience for these kinds of events. Not on a regular basis. But it is a part of this business."

She nodded slowly. "I understand that."

"Business comes first for you as well," he said. "I can tell you take work very seriously."

"Having a job is important, necessary. Having a great job is icing on the cake. And having a job I love that garners lots of positive publicity…there isn't anything more satisfying. So, yes, business comes first."

"You enjoy the publicity?"

It was nice to see her name in a magazine without a sleazy innuendo connected to it. Nice to have her name associated with something she was proud of. Although, she always hoped people thought she was a different Madeline Forrester. Really she just hoped they didn't think of the earlier stories about her at all.

"Yes. It's been great for my professional reputation."

"Why work so hard to build a public reputation? Unless you're planning on branching off on your own?"

"Maybe. Eventually. Not now," she said, breathless, knowing she'd just said the wrong thing. "I mean, perhaps in ten years' time…"

His dark brows locked together. "You're planning on leaving Petrova?"

"I'm not planning anything. Not really. Well, maybe.

But do you honestly expect that I'm going to work for you for the rest of my life? I have ambition." She looked back down at her shoes.

"What's wrong with working for me?" he asked, his voice soft, smooth, but she could hear the hard note beneath all that civility.

"Nothing. But did you want to be someone's employee for the rest of your life?"

"That's different."

"It's not," she insisted.

"I thought you were the best in the business," he said. "So either you're willing to hand Petrova Gems over to someone who does subpar work, or you lied about your skills."

She narrowed her eyes and pushed off from the wall, not caring, for the moment, that it brought them closer together.

"I am the best. Maybe you can contract my company to do your events and exhibits."

"Your plan is to create your own business co-ordinating events?"

"Yes."

Aleksei felt a surge of annoyance rush through his veins. He had hired Madeline when she'd had very little experience in the way of event planning, and she was intent upon taking that knowledge and applying it somewhere else.

He looked at her, so petite and pretty in her dress. Her eyes full of fear and determination.

"And you feel you could handle the responsibility of running your own company?" he asked.

"I majored in Business."

"A worthless degree in my opinion. You either have what it takes to make it, or you don't."

"Inspirational. You should speak at high school graduations."

A rusty chuckle climbed his throat. Her wit and boldness always impressed him. The fact that she had a viewpoint and her own opinions was one of the reasons he'd hired her.

He'd always enjoyed that in their phone conversations. It was nice having someone ready to engage in a verbal battle when he was in a bad mood, or when he simply needed the challenge. Very few people would dare talk to him like Madeline did. All of that deference got old after a while. Especially when he'd realized what an illusion it was. After he'd realized that none of it meant anything.

"Do you know, I had considered that? But they don't like it when you tell them skip college and get a job."

"Did you?"

College had been nothing more than a fantasy. Finishing high school had been beyond his reach. He'd always had to work. But he didn't resent it. It had made him hard enough to withstand the struggle required to succeed. There had been one bright spot in his life. And then tragedy had extinguished the only light he'd ever known, leaving wounds that had scarred over into granite.

"I had no other option. But I didn't need another option."

She bit into her lush bottom lip, leaving a row of even marks. He fought the urge to extend his hand, to soothe away the impressions with his thumb. "My brother made me go to college."

"Your brother?"

She lowered her eyes, an annoying habit she seemed to be developing. "He's…he's very successful and he wanted to make sure that I was successful too."

She was holding back. He shouldn't care. And yet he found he wanted to know the secret she had nearly let slip. The one she didn't want to tell him.

He did not know why he felt compelled to learn her secrets, only that he did. He shouldn't have even felt the need to follow her out into the hall. And yet when he'd seen her petite figure weaving through the crowd, he had started following.

"So your brother is the one who ensured you got your degree?"

She nodded. "Yes. He has one too, and he owns a massive chain of very successful resorts. So…not so worthless."

He chuckled, surprising himself as much as he surprised her. "I do know who your brother is."

He noticed a flood of red creeping up her neck and into her cheeks. "Of course you do. He's been extremely successful. All my family has been."

"And you needed to keep up?"

"Maybe I just needed to be more famous than the rest of them," she said, a slow smile spreading over her face, while her blush still lingered.

"Somehow, you don't strike me as that type."

She raised perfectly groomed brows. "I don't?"

"No. You practically ran out of the ballroom earlier, so you don't seem as though you're courting fame to me."

"Okay, maybe it's not about fame. I just want to have success on my own."

Her tongue darted out and she slicked it over her bottom lip. He couldn't stop himself from watching the movement, couldn't stop himself from imagining touching his own tongue to that luscious mouth.

She was a very desirable woman. And he hadn't had sex in a long time. He had left Olivia neglected in Milan for a good five months before he had ended the relationship.

"Ambitious," he said.

She looked up at him, blue eyes wide. "What's life without a goal?"

"Boring," he responded.

"Exactly," she said.

He moved nearer to her, so close he could smell the woman beneath the floral perfume. "We are like-minded in some ways then."

She swayed slightly, as though she might be tempted to close the distance between them.

"Strange." She swallowed, and instead of moving closer, he felt her retreat slightly. "Ah…maybe you should circulate some more. And I have to…uh… The shrimp."

"Shrimp?"

"The buffet. It's low on shrimp."

He inclined his head. "Then I'll let you get to that, and I'll circulate."

She walked past him, soft curves brushing against him. His body reacted. Viscerally. Hungrily.

A shame he had chosen to cut ties with his mistress. A shame he hadn't called one of the models, or chatted up one of the women in the ballroom. Now there would be no taking the edge off his need anytime in the near future. His body rebelled at the thought anyway.

Olivia wasn't the woman he wanted. Neither were any of women in the ballroom. Not tonight.

"Don't you…? I mean…you were going to go and…" She made a sweeping gesture with her hand.

"Yes, circulate. I'm clear on that. Are you dismissing me?"

She shook her head and her glossy ponytail swung in time with the motion. "No, not at all."

"Because it's bad business to dismiss your boss," he said.

He moved toward her, so close that all he would have to do was wrap an arm around her waist and pull her in to join his lips to hers.

"I'm sure it's bad business to linger alone in empty hallways with your boss too," she said, her eyes fixed on his lips, her expression mesmerized.

"Likely," he said.

Their eyes clashed and held.

"Very bad business," she said softly, before turning away from him.

"I'll talk to you soon, Madeline," he said.

Maddy turned and headed toward the kitchen, her heart hammering in her ears. It was disconcerting to realize that she had so much weakness in her. To realize that men were her weakness. She wasn't tempted as long as she was avoiding them. But it seemed like whenever she was put into close proximity with one…

She braced her hand on the wall and slowed her breathing, trying to clear her head. No, men weren't her weakness. She had just been faced head on with the fact that she was suffering severe sexual deprivation—something she hadn't been conscious of when there wasn't an attractive man around.

Soon things would go back to the way they'd been. They would go back to communicating over the phone and the computer and she would be free of the disturbing effect her boss had on her when they were in the same room together.

She wouldn't have to face the weakness that still lived inside of her.

CHAPTER FOUR

EVERY time Maddy saw a positive headline with her name attached to it, it helped to erase some of the lingering sting left by her experience with the media five years earlier. And this morning, she had a fantastic headline to look at.

The party had been a complete success and the pieces in Aleksei's collection were set to be the must-have items of the year. Of course, most people would only be able to afford the mass-produced pieces, and not the handmade originals. The originals would sell for upwards of a million dollars at auction at the end of the exhibition tour.

Her cellphone rang and she snatched it up from the vanity top. "Madeline Forrester."

"Good work last night, Madeline."

Her stomach dropped to her toes. "Thank you, Mr. Petrov." She sneaked a glance at her own reflection in the mirror and saw that her cheeks were glowing pink.

She tried, valiantly, not to picture what Aleksei might be doing.

"Preparing to head to Switzerland yet?"

"I got a late checkout. My train doesn't leave until two. The ballroom at the Appenzell is easily twice as big as the one here, so I need to start prep work early."

"Why don't you ride with me, rather than taking the two o'clock?"

"With you?" she asked, parroting.

"I leave at noon and I have a private car reserved. Better than riding in one of the public cars, I would think."

She looked at her reflection head on this time, disgusted by the color in her face and the glitter in her eyes. She was excited. Excited to see him again.

No way was she riding with him. She wasn't spending anymore time with him than was necessary, not until she got a grip on herself again.

"We can talk more about where you plan on being in ten years, professionally, and how we might be able to work your long-term goals into a position at Petrova."

Suddenly, riding with him seemed like a pretty big necessity. Because if she didn't, if she let the attraction she felt for him do potential damage to her career, then she might as well just jump him and ruin her career that way.

She wasn't about to do either. She certainly wasn't going to let fear and insecurity hold her back in her professional life.

"Excellent, what time do you want me to meet you?"

"Meet me in the lobby at eleven and we can share a car to the train station."

"Great, see you then."

When she hung up the phone and set it back down on the vanity top, she realized how tightly she'd been gripping it, how hard she'd had it pressed to her ear. She rubbed at the sore spot near her temple.

A trickle of excitement moved through her, picking up steam as it went. It was because of the possibility of promotion, or eventual promotion. Nothing to do with seeing Aleksei again.

She ground her teeth together as she crossed the room and started flinging her belongings into her suitcase.

Yes, it did have to do with seeing Aleksei again. There. Honesty.

But she didn't want it to have anything to do with him. Didn't want to be curious about what kind of man he was, or what he might look like out of his perfectly tailored suits. The fact that she'd entertained the thought of him undressed at all made her feel…it made her feel dirty.

The fact that she wanted him, that she was attracted to him, made her feel unclean in some way. If she could just ignore her sex drive, she would. And in all honesty, and for the most part, she did ignore it.

And she would just keep ignoring it. Problem solved.

She closed the suitcase lid and pressed hard on it, clicking the locks into place. She didn't have the luxury of hanging around angsting about her own issues. She was moving on, moving forward. That was how she'd been living every day since she was twenty-two and it was how she would keep living.

She wasn't going to allow her mistakes to keep her stuck somewhere. She'd worked hard to get where she was. After her very public fall from grace she'd had to work at horrible catering jobs, awful party-planning companies, doing the worst grunt work, so that she could build up a résumé impressive enough to get hired at the North American branch of Petrova. And she'd worked hard to get promoted and moved to the Milan office a couple of months ago. She wasn't stopping now.

She wasn't going to allow anything, least of all an attraction for her boss, to keep her from reaching her full potential at Petrova Gems.

And if that meant she had to sit across from Aleksei Petrov and talk to him while she tried desperately not to imagine what it would be like to reach out and touch the rough, black stubble of his five o'clock shadow then she would do just that.

Aleksei hadn't been in the lobby to meet her. Which was actually a huge relief. Instead, his driver had been there, sending Aleksei's regrets that he'd had a matter to see to in one of the Milan showrooms.

Her reprieve was temporary, since he was meeting her at the train station, but still, she'd take what she could get.

When they arrived at the train station, Aleksei's driver ushered her from the car and escorted her to Aleksei's private railcar.

Well, without Aleksei, it was a no-brainer how she'd rather travel. The space was large and luxurious, with plush couches and a dining set. The domed ceilings were painted a rich blue and gold trim framed the large windows, designed to give the passengers an unsurpassed view of whatever landscape they were passing through.

It didn't even compare to the cramped seating in a public car. Now, if only she didn't have to share it with Aleksei…

"Good, you made it."

Think of the devil.

She turned and her heart lurched. "Uh…yes, your driver was very accommodating."

Aleksei raised a dark eyebrow. "Good. I apologize that I couldn't meet you."

"You don't have to apologize."

"I know," he said. "But I did."

"Impeccable manners."

"Sometimes."

A small laugh bubbled in her throat and escaped her lips. He made her laugh. He really needed to stop doing that.

"Would you like to have a seat?" He gestured to the long cream couch that stretched across most of the room.

She set her bright pink purse on the floor and sat down on the thick-cushioned couch. Oh, yes, she could get used to this.

"Coffee?" he asked.

"Oh, always," she said.

He pushed an intercom button by the door and spoke quickly in Italian. She lived in Milan now, had for two months, but she was a long way from mastering the language. Aleksei spoke at least three languages. That sort of proficiency was intimidating to be around.

He took a seat across from her in one of the big, dark leather chairs.

"So, what's this about job opportunities?" she asked, trying to disguise the eager note in her voice.

"What are you interested in?"

"What am I…? What do I want to do?"

"Yes. We're just having a discussion, Madeline. You're the one with the ten-year plan. What do you need to feel satisfied with Petrova Gems in ten years?"

He leaned back in the chair, long legs stretched in front of him. She noticed the way his pants pulled tight, revealing muscular thighs. His build was total perfection. He was, hands down, the most gorgeous man she'd ever seen. Black hair, olive skin, sensual lips that she knew could soften for a real smile, even if she'd never seen it.

There was something wrong with her head.

The door to the private compartment opened and a man in a suit wheeled a trolley in with coffee, cream and an assortment of things to sweeten the drink. She thanked him—that much Italian she could manage—and started fixing her coffee, keeping her focus on her cup, and off the man currently melting her brain.

"So this is…anything I want?" she asked when she settled back onto the couch.

"This is hypothetical, but it has the possibility of becoming more."

She felt her face get hot as his words took on an unintended meaning. She took a sip of coffee. "Well, I like the artistic aspect of the event-planning. I like the smaller shows too, dealing with the art galleries and the museums. But, I really like the marketing aspects. I majored in Business—" she ignored the look that he gave her and pressed on "—but I did a minor in Market Research and Advertising. I find that part of the business interesting."

"And if I moved you into Marketing you would stay?"

"Hypothetically," she said, taking another sip of coffee, "I could do that on my own too."

"But not for me. I don't hire out for as many things as possible. I like to work with the same people, within my company, and have as much control of it as possible."

Which she could understand. And it sounded worse when he said it than it actually was. He was a good boss. A great one. Especially when he wasn't three feet away. Yes, most especially then.

"And on your own…you lack job security. Security of any kind, really. It's a competitive field. At least, it is if you're attempting success rather than mediocrity, which I assume you are."

She swallowed a scalding mouthful of coffee. "Naturally."

"In which case staying with Petrova is a better option."

She set her mug down on the trolley and leaned forward. "So…you actually want to keep me on?"

"You're a valuable employee, Madeline."

A rush of pleasure moved through her veins. Being appreciated was foreign in so many ways. For a moment, she simply enjoyed it. She didn't put a wall up, didn't try to shield herself from her feelings. She'd learned to filter things, good and bad, to protect herself. But she could enjoy this, enjoy that Aleksei Petrov was fighting to keep her on staff.

Could enjoy being wanted. Needed.

"Thank you."

She was actually choked up. Why did affirmation from him mean anything? She should be fine on her own. She shouldn't need a pat on the back from him, or anyone.

But it felt really, really good. And it was tempting to just feel good for a while.

"I have owned my own company long enough to know that, no matter how good I am at what I do, if I'm not surrounded by employees that are as committed and as skilled, true success is not possible," he said.

It was a rare thing, she knew, to have a boss that actually appreciated the work that was done in the trenches and not only that, a boss who didn't see employees as expendable.

At her very first office job, an internship, she'd been so cloistered in her boss's domain she'd got a very good idea that he didn't respect anyone who worked for him. Of course, she hadn't seen it that way; she'd eaten up his explanations of why everyone was incompetent. He'd appreciated her, so he'd said. And she had been... so needy. And so very, very stupid.

She'd allowed that—his proclamation of all other workers at the company as morons—to cut her off from her coworkers. To isolate her. Which had been William's aim, of course. Keep her separate, keep her ignorant. And she had been more than willing to walk right into that trap.

A reminder of why she wasn't going to sit around and indulge in warm fuzzies now.

Although, at least Aleksei acknowledged the hard work of everyone in the company. Not just the designers or the management. And not just an innocent young intern.

"I...well, I really appreciate that you consider me a valuable member of the team. And it isn't like I was planning on leaving Petrova tomorrow."

"When it becomes something you're seriously considering, talk to me."

"I will."

She leaned back, letting the soft cushions take some

of the tension out of her shoulders, letting the silence stretch between them.

"You don't want coffee?" she asked.

He shook his head. "I dislike the idea of depending on anything that alters my mood."

Now he did, anyway. Aleksei had come too close, had been too tempted to simply drown himself in a bottle of alcohol when Paulina had died. Had done for a while. It had been easier not to feel. Now, he didn't need a substance to accomplish that. It simply came naturally to him.

But that was why his business was so important. He didn't rely on caffeine, or alcohol. He relied on success. The high of being the best. Of knocking out competition. Becoming the most recognized brand name in jewelry. He had done all of that.

Now he was simply working for more. More success. More wealth. But he had to keep moving. Because when he stopped…well, he just didn't stop. He hadn't, not since that first low. Not since he'd determined he wouldn't let himself sink into oblivion, not matter how much he wanted to.

He very much wasn't in oblivion now, and the arousal coursing through his body when he looked at Madeline was a reminder of that.

He didn't sleep with employees. It was bad for business, and it was shameless abuse of power. He believed that. He lived by it. But Madeline tested that. Was a temptation beyond anything he had known before.

It was six years since his wife had died. Since he had watched them lower the casket, holding the woman he loved, into the ground. A part of him had been buried then too.

He'd had sex since then, of course. After the physical need had come back, he'd taken care of it. Long-term mistresses being his solution of choice.

But what he felt was basic sexual arousal, a man responding to a woman. Any woman. But it wasn't unique. There was no fire.

When he looked at Madeline, there was fire. Heat and desire on a level he couldn't remember feeling before. The need was for her. The fire burned for her. Not for Olivia. Not for some anonymous woman.

Not even for his wife.

He clenched his hands tight, until the tendons stretched, the mild pain a hope of distraction from the current of need that was washing through him. It didn't work.

Not with her so close, glossy brown hair tumbling over her shoulders in waves, blue eyes bright, the pale, lush curve of her breasts framed by the scoop neck of her deep purple top. She was a call to sin he didn't know if he wanted to resist.

He could. He was certain of that. He'd been to hell and back in his life. Willpower, strength wasn't an issue. But he wasn't sure he wanted to turn away.

The only thing that made him question it wasn't her status at the company—somewhere in the past ten minutes he'd gotten over that—it was the haunted look she got in those beautiful blue eyes. A look he didn't want to take on. A look he didn't want to contribute to.

She sighed and leaned back, berry-stained lips curving into a soft smile. "I should probably adopt your philosophy. Or maybe start sleeping. But there's always so much to do and…coffee's more readily available than downtime."

"I don't really sleep anyway," he said.

He hadn't slept through the night since Paulina died. But it was good. He used that. He worked. He kept his mind busy.

"I wish I didn't need sleep," she said, misunderstanding.

Good. He didn't wish that sort of nightmarish insomnia on anyone. Living between sleep and being awake, with only ghosts for company.

"There are advantages," he said. "Especially as we have shops in so many time zones, offices in so many time zones. It helps that I'm able to get up and make calls when I need to."

"Mmm," she said absently, sipping her coffee, slender fingers sliding over the ceramic handle of the mug. Which shouldn't be arousing, not in any way. And yet, it was.

It was far too easy to imagine those smooth, delicate hands caressing his body.

When he looked at her eyes again, they were intent on him, the glitter in them hot, longing. Her cheeks flushed with color. Need. Want. Desire. He saw it all there. He saw it because it reflected what he felt.

He met her gaze, dared her to look away. She didn't. But then she blinked and brought down the shutters, her eyes blank of anything other than sheer stubbornness.

Aleksei knew women. He created jewelry for women, to make them feel beautiful, to make them happy. It wasn't often he felt he didn't understand a woman's thoughts.

Madeline continued to look at him, her expression cool now. As if trying to prove to him that he was wrong about the fire he was certain he'd glimpsed.

He was more accustomed to women making invitations, to them following up a moment of clear physical attraction with an attempt at making it more than simple attraction.

It was clear Madeline was not going to be making any invitations.

"When you're ready, Madeline," he said, "we can discuss what it is you want."

Her eyes widened, her cheeks flushing. "With work?"

He couldn't suppress the rush of pure satisfaction that flooded through him. "Of course."

She nodded. "Yes…that sounds…good."

His heart was pounding faster, adrenaline pumping through his veins. Blood running hotter and faster as he imagined what it would be like to get her to confess her desire for him. Interest. Excitement. Feeling. After six years of experiencing nothing more than basic human needs, this was foreign to him.

He wanted Madeline Forrester. And he intended to have her.

"Oh, please be straight," Maddy muttered under her breath as she finished tacking up part of the large swath of silk fabric.

She was trying to make a swag effect around the ballroom between the wall and the ceiling in an attempt to soften what was a very crisp look. All of the decorations, the table settings, the linens, the lights, would be white, and the idea was to add texture and dimension.

Which was why she was wobbling on the second-from-the-top rung of a ladder, hanging on with one hand and trying to wrangle the fabric with the others.

"What the *hell* are you doing?" Aleksei's deep voice resonated in the empty ballroom.

Maddy wobbled a bit and set the last tack into place, covering it carefully with a fold of fabric, before looking down.

"Working," she said sharply. "And could you not sneak up on me when I'm nine feet off the ground?"

She moved her foot forward, careful not to snag her high heel on the ladder rungs as she climbed down. Her shoe slipped on the last rung and she gripped the sides of the ladder tightly, making a very ungraceful dismount as she plopped both feet on the marble floor.

Her heart was pounding heavily, from the almost fall and from Aleksei's presence. She'd managed to avoid him in the two days since the train ride from Milan. Since the moment she'd nearly given in to the desire coursing through her and touched him. She'd been so tempted. So weak.

She turned and took a step back and nearly ran into Aleksei's broad, muscular body. He reached out and bracketed her in, his hands gripping both sides of the ladder.

"What were you doing?" he asked, voice low and deadly.

"My job," she said stiffly, trying to fight the languor that was spreading through her.

"You were on top of a ladder in high-heeled shoes. Do you have any idea how dangerous that is?"

"No. I mean, maybe it is a little, but I work in heels a lot, and I climb ladders sometimes."

"Don't I pay a very efficient team to help you with the physical aspects of preparing for events?" he practically growled.

"Yes, you do, but I was experimenting with this effect and sometimes it's just easier to execute an idea myself. I'm not always sure how it will come together and…"

"It was a very foolish thing to do."

He was so very close. And he was angry, but he wasn't scary. He was concerned…for her. And that was…that was almost more intoxicating than being close enough to him that with the slightest tilt of her head she could brush her lips against his.

She jerked her head back, because if she didn't do that, she was going to do the opposite. And that would be beyond stupid.

But then he moved his hand, placed it on her back. His large, warm palm spread wide across her shoulder-blades, heat seeping through her silk blouse. He moved his thumb slightly, the faint rasp of calluses against the thin fabric audible in the large, empty space.

Everything in her was tangled. Snarled together so tightly that she was immobilized by it. She couldn't do anything but stand there and stare at him. Part of her wanted to move away. To run, as fast as she could. Away from the job, from the man. From the temptation. From the sneaky little hussy that lived inside of her that wanted everything she should never, ever have.

But so much of her wanted to stay. To revel in that touch. The woman in her wanted it, wanted his hands to slide over her body, for the touch to become intimate.

It wasn't normal to be celibate for so long. It just wasn't. And she wanted…she just *wanted*. And really, wasn't that normal? To want a man to want her? To want the man in return? It was hard to have a healthy view on your sexuality when the press had labeled you a home-wrecking slut. It was hard not to see yourself that way. At least, it was hard for her.

And that was why, for five years, there hadn't been anyone. Not a lover, not even a date. No kissing, no caressing. There was no middle ground in her life. There had been work. That was all.

That wasn't right. It wasn't right that she'd let William and his deceit dictate her actions for so long. He never should have had that power. Never should have had any power at all.

But he did. Even with the realization, he still did.

She moved away from Aleksei, and he let her go. "I'm fine," she said, her voice hard. "And I wouldn't have lost my balance at all if you hadn't come in and yelled at me, so maybe next time wait until my feet are on the ground before you come after me."

He strode toward her, his expression fierce. "Is this a joke to you? Do you know how quickly things end? Do you understand?"

The rawness in his voice shocked her. The depth of emotion. She honestly didn't want to know where it came from. She couldn't handle it. If she knew who he was, beyond being a good boss, if there was any more... she just couldn't.

"I'm sorry," she said, needing to defuse it. "I'll be more careful next time. I'll wear better shoes."

"Have one of the other staff do it."

"Why? They aren't any more smash-proof than I am."

His dark eyes were hard, uncompromising. "Have one of the other staff do it."

He was her boss. Something she needed to remember. "Okay, next time I'll have one of the team do it. Does that satisfy you?"

A muscle in his jaw jumped. "I'm as close to satisfied as I will get," he said stiffly, walking ahead of her and out of the room.

She put her hand over her heart, felt it beating rapidly beneath her palm. She didn't know what had just happened. What had passed between them. What had changed. But something had.

And she knew that there would be no putting things back as they had been.

CHAPTER FIVE

PERFECT. It was all perfect. From the glossy white floors to the white silk draping from the ceiling, Madeline had executed the look of the ballroom with style and grace. It was classic, with a modern edge.

Of course, Madeline had nearly broken her neck for the effect.

It was possible he'd overreacted. When he'd walked into the ballroom and seen her there, nine feet above the marble floor, three inch spiked heels draped over the ladder rungs, the rush of anger and adrenaline that had filled him had been instant.

He would have reacted to any employee, any person, behaving so recklessly. Of course, she hadn't seen her behavior as reckless. Stubborn woman.

"Aleksei." The woman next to him, a woman whose name he hadn't bothered to get, stroked his forearm with long, manicured fingers. "I do so enjoy every piece that you've designed. I have a fabulous idea for your next collection."

He let her drone on. He didn't need ideas, especially not from spoiled heiresses.

Then he caught sight of Madeline. Madeline who was wrapped up tight in a slinky, form-fitting white dress that conjured up fantasies that were hardly pure. Madeline, who had caused him to remain sleepless every night of the week. She was slipping out the side door, making her escape, just as she had done at the Milan exhibition. He was done with sleepless nights. He was done wanting and not having.

He set the champagne glass down on one of the tables and extricated himself from the other woman's hold. She was still talking to anyone who would listen as he made his way across the ballroom and to the door that was nearest him.

It would only take a taste. Something to satisfy the hunger that was eating at him. If he could have that, if he could satisfy his curiosity…that was all he needed.

He looked down the corridor and saw the tail of Madeline's white dress disappear as she exited the hall and went to the indoor gardens.

It had been a long time since he'd pursued a woman, if he ever had. He didn't usually bother. But this woman had burrowed her way under his skin. Until he had her, until he sated his body's desire for her, she would seem like so much more than she was.

She was just a woman. He was a man. They wanted each other. It was that basic. It was nothing more. He just needed to prove that to his body.

She was standing near the door when he walked in, her attention fixed on some of the tropical plants. A striking contrast, the bright pink flowers, Madeline in white, and the deep snow just outside the warm glass sanctuary that shielded all the delicate blooms.

He took a moment to admire her, admire the small dip of her waist, the curve of her hip. Especially that tight round bottom, a feature that made him wonder if she spent time in the gym.

She turned suddenly. "Aleksei," she said, no emotion to her voice.

"You're always running out on your own events. If you don't enjoy them, you might worry about the guests."

Soft pink lips tilted up half-heartedly. "Well, last time I had to get shrimp."

"That's right."

"And this time...I needed...air." She looked away from him and turned her focus to the thick glass walls. "I didn't need it bad enough to go out there and brave the snow so I thought I would compromise."

"You look tired," he said. It was true. There were shadows under her eyes, but it was more than that, it was in the way she held herself. He didn't like to see it. It made him feel...responsible somehow.

She pulled her lips into a hard line. "I don't know that that's an appropriate thing for a boss to say."

He took a step closer to her. "And a friend?"

"You aren't my friend."

No. He wasn't. Anything he said to her, any personal gesture he made, would be made with the aim of getting her into bed. That wasn't the action of a friend. Though, truly he wasn't certain that he had friends. He certainly hadn't gone out of his way to cultivate any friendships. He had never been the social one.

"True." He watched her face, the way she looked at him. The hungry look in her eyes, the one that mirrored his own growing need. "Are you going to pretend there's nothing more between us than a working relationship?"

She pulled her mouth tighter, into a determined

pucker. "Yes, I think I should pretend that. Because what's the point of going anywhere else?"

He moved closer to her, half expecting her to back away, but she didn't. She held her ground, arms at her sides.

"Nothing long-term," he said. "But there are benefits to short-term arrangements."

"The woman you were talking to?"

"No one. I didn't even ask her name."

Madeline only looked at him for a moment, clenching and unclenching her fists, shifting her weight from one foot to the other. She stepped forward and put her hands on his cheeks, blue eyes serious as she looked at him. Then she pulled up on her toes and kissed him.

Her kiss was clumsy, a bit inexperienced, but her enthusiasm more than made up for any missing skill. She kissed like a woman who was starving, and he was more than willing to meet her need.

He wrapped his arm around her waist and pulled her to him, groaned when he felt her full breasts press against his chest. Her tongue, soft and wet, slicked against his lips, a timid question in its touch. And he answered, meeting her thrust for thrust, tasting, savoring, enjoying every bit of her sweet mouth.

An enthusiastic sound climbed her throat and vibrated between their lips as she shifted her hands so that she was clinging to his shoulders. He cupped the back of her head with his other hand, sifting his fingers through silky strands.

Just a taste? He wanted a feast. Wanted to move his hands over her curves, without the thin barrier of her dress hindering him. He wanted to feel her skin, smooth and warm. Wanted to taste every inch of her.

As suddenly as she'd started the kiss, she pulled away. And he let her go, watching her. Her eyes were wide, her lips swollen, cheeks flushed, her breasts rising and falling harshly with each breath.

She pushed a hand through her thoroughly mussed hair. "I had to…I had to see," she said, her voice shaky.

"You had to see?" he asked, his own voice roughened by arousal.

"I thought it couldn't possibly be as good as I imagined. It never is, you know."

"And?"

She cursed and turned away from him.

"That good?" he asked.

She turned back to face him. "I can't," she said simply. "It's unprofessional."

"We passed unprofessional a while ago, I think."

"Yes, okay, we did. But continuing would be…more unprofessional."

She stood back and looked at him, her eyes hard, as if she was waiting for something. Waiting for him to grab her, or…he didn't know what else. He knew it went with the wariness he saw in her eyes sometimes. Knew he didn't want to take it on. He couldn't be anyone's knight in shining armor. Didn't want to be.

"All right, Madeline, if you don't want to, that's your decision. I don't coerce women into bed. I don't have to. But I know you feel the attraction. You've proved it. And as far as professional goes, the line has been crossed with or without actual sex."

She shook her head, dark curls bouncing with the motion. "Office stuff is complicated. I have too much tied up in this job." Her eyes narrowed. "You aren't going to fire me if I say no, are you?"

"I told you, I don't do coercion, and that encompasses asking someone to prostitute herself for a job. I can be ruthless in matters of business, but I do not abuse people."

Madeline swallowed, but her throat remained dry. She'd just made the second biggest mistake of her life. Okay, possibly third biggest, but it was still big. She never should have kissed him. Ever.

But fantasy never lived up to reality and she'd been so desperate to purge the desire for Aleksei from her system, to do something to get the reckless ache to desert her. She'd been sick with jealousy watching that woman caress his arm and whisper in his ear. It wasn't emotional jealousy, it was basic, physical jealousy. She didn't want another woman to have what she was so set on denying herself.

And with that desire came guilt that was nearly crippling. Guilt because she wanted a man, for the first time in five years. Guilt because she couldn't repress her sexuality anymore. Guilt because she still wanted sex when she'd been so convinced she could let that part of herself go. When she'd been so convinced that she should. Because how could she ever trust herself again?

And then she'd thought, as he was standing there looking so gorgeous it made her body hurt with desire, that she could prove it wouldn't really be electric. She had limited experience with men, only one miserable lover to her credit, and the physical side of things had never been so incredible for her. It had been about emotions, not any kind of true desire.

But Aleksei's kiss had sent a current through her body that had immobilized her with its strength. Had melted her with its heat. She'd meant to close the door on it. Had meant to remind her body that all that physical stuff wasn't everything it was made out to be.

Except it had been more. More than she'd imagined and more than it had ever been for her.

Counterproductive.

"I'm sure you don't." She believed him. Believed that he didn't get his kicks out of abusing his power. He hadn't tried to talk her into it. Hadn't said how beautiful she was. Hadn't said he loved her.

He hadn't lied. And she had kissed him. And lightning hadn't struck her dead on the spot. There was no scarlet letter out in the snow.

That was all very good to know.

"I just can't…" It was too easy to remember what had happened last time. And it was her boss again, for heaven's sake. Although, if there was a similarity between Aleksei and William she couldn't think of it.

"It's not a good idea," she finished.

"It's not," he agreed.

She folded her arms under her breasts, because she was cold. Because she needed a shield. She put her head down and walked past him, heading to the door.

When he spoke again, his voice was soft, but commanding. "It's not a good idea. But I want you. If you want this to happen, you have to come to me now, Madeline. I'm not playing games, and I don't chase after women."

She didn't turn. "I won't change my mind. I can't."

It crushed part of her to say that. To be such a coward. Because there was common sense involved, yes, but most of it was just fear. And she hated that she was the sort of person who let fear have a hand in her life.

But it was too strong, too real, for her to fight.

He moved so that he was behind her, pushed the door open and held it for her. "And that is your decision. It remains your decision." He didn't believe her. Of course he didn't. She didn't believe herself. "Can I escort you back to the ballroom?"

She nodded stiffly. The best thing to do would be to pretend nothing had happened.

That she'd never felt his tongue slide against hers. Never been held in his strong arms.

She could do it. She could go back to the way things had been. She wasn't weak. At least, she wouldn't be anymore.

"Hello, Madeline." Aleksei's smooth voice was more torturous now than it had ever been. Now that she'd tasted his lips. Felt his hands, rough and insistent on her. Rough and insistent in a good way. In the way that made a woman feel want at the exclusion of everything else.

"Hello," she responded, her voice coming out short and crisp.

"How is everything shaping up for the exhibition in Luxembourg?"

She leaned back in her chair and arched her back, stretching out her knotted muscles. "Great. Better than great. We have use of the entire castle, which means on the invites I'm going to have guests check whether or not they would like the use of a room in the castle for the night, and to join us for a gourmet breakfast the next morning."

"Extravagant."

"You can afford it," she said.

"Of course."

It was the perfect venue as far as she was concerned.

It was turning into the largest event for this collection, and she was very happy with it. The guest list included some of the world's wealthiest and most influential people, and the setting was designed to impress.

"I'd also like to display some pieces from your past collections if there are originals still available."

"Some, although most have been sold at auction."

"Whatever we can get our hands on. Since we have use of the whole space, I want to use the whole space."

She could do this. It was easy to talk work with Aleksei. They meshed there. They connected. On this one plane of existence they connected. And it was really the only way they needed to connect.

Yes, it was. No need to connect in any other way. Not at the lips or…anywhere else.

She grimaced and leaned forward, picking up a pen so she could take notes or something. Anything to keep her mind fully occupied so that it didn't go off on tangents about connecting to Aleksei.

It was better with hundreds of miles between them. Better with the barrier of the phone. She wished, she wished so much, that they had never broken that barrier. It would all be simpler. She wouldn't be having sleepless nights dreaming about his touch, wouldn't get hot every time his name was mentioned in conversation.

"I'm stopping by later today," he said. "We can discuss it further then."

She stood up. "What?" He never came to the Milan office. Well, not in the two months since she'd been there, which didn't really equate to never. But he certainly didn't come often. He'd been in Moscow and she'd been perfectly happy with him there.

"You're looking forward to it, I can tell," he said drily.

"Sorry." She shook her head and cursed herself inwardly. She would kill for a little sexual sophistication right about now. Sadly, she wasn't going to get it in the next hour.

Though she was getting to the point where she was really thinking it was time. She'd allowed herself to be tied up in the horror from five years ago for a long time. Too long. Longer than her former boss, certainly. Likely longer than her former boss's ex-wife. The media didn't even care anymore, hadn't for a long time.

But her name had been synonymous with slut for a good two months. Her brother had done his absolute best to protect her. His misguided best since she'd sworn to him that nothing had happened. A huge weight she carried still.

It was easy to make excuses. For all of it. For lying to Gage—she was embarrassed, humiliated, and, no, of course she hadn't known her boss was married. For any of it happening in the first place—William had said he loved her. But the fact was, there wasn't an excuse. She'd been stupid, she'd been naive and she'd allowed herself to be manipulated.

An affection-starved young woman, barely a woman, who had lapped up every compliment, every ounce of affection her boss had sent her way.

But she was still letting that man manipulate her, and it was a fair bet he couldn't even remember her name. He had likely replaced her, and the wife he'd lost over the affair he'd had with her, ten times over by now.

And she was still stuck. Still wallowing in all the pain and regret of the past. All that moving on and up nonsense was just that. It was a lie. To herself and to everyone else.

Being with Aleksei, sleeping with him, might not be a good idea. But her decision about it shouldn't hinge on things in the past. It should just hinge on the fact that a workplace dalliance wasn't really the brightest move of all time.

"I'll…I'll see you soon then," she said.

She hung the phone up and sat back down. Her heart was pounding hard, her hands shaking. And this time, it wasn't all Aleksei's doing.

She'd had a breakthrough. In ten minutes. She hadn't put her relationship with William behind her. She hadn't moved on. She was letting him control her life, even now.

And it was ending today.

CHAPTER SIX

OF COURSE, Aleksei hadn't simply stopped by. He'd stayed the entire day. And of course, the reason for his visit had been the next exhibition.

Which meant she was involved. In every aspect of his visit. The large staff meeting, the smaller staff meeting, and now she was cloistered in his office after-hours with him, and they were hashing out details between the two of them.

Usually, Aleksei left her job to her. Of course, the exhibitions she'd planned in North America had been less crucial. But this exhibition, this collection was personal to him, for obvious reasons, and he was right in the middle of everything, putting in his own thoughts, changing things around and generally disturbing her.

"So what do we want to do with the necklace?" she asked.

The necklace being the secret piece of Aleksei's new collection. An emerald, diamond and platinum creation that, just in materials, was worth half a million dollars. With Aleksei as the designer, the creator of the piece, it was worth much more. And he had been holding it back for this portion of the tour.

The buzz about the exhibition was already electric.

"I think it should be there when the guests arrive. I want it to be the centerpiece of the show, in the middle of things, but secure."

"Well, we can put alarms around it without obstructing the view of the display case. And of course we'll have security guards. Everywhere." She leaned back in the office chair and stretched her neck. "And then, when the actual event is over, and the guests that are staying in the rooms overnight retire, we'll take the jewels away in the armored cars."

They'd never had a theft attempt, but Aleksei believed in being vigilant. Which was probably why there had never been a theft attempt.

"That all sounds good," he said, standing from his desk and rounding it, coming to stand in front of her.

At five foot three, she wasn't tall, not by any stretch of the imagination, which was why she always gave herself a boost with high heels. But Aleksei was easily a foot taller. And so broad and masculine. He made her feel small, petite. Feminine. The strangest thing was that she sort of liked it.

She blinked, trying to refocus her mind.

She bent down to get her purse before standing. The motion brought her a little closer to him than she'd anticipated. It suddenly felt much hotter in the room.

He was looking at her, dark eyes trained on her face, then dipping to her lips. The tension was thick, physical, like a wire that had been stretched between them had been tightened. Tightened to the point where she felt sure it would break.

Breathing was nearly impossible. "Anything else?" she asked. She needed to escape. Now. Badly.

But she also wanted to stay. Wanted to find out what

would happen if things kept going. She wanted to see what it would take to make the wire snap.

"Only this." He leaned, dipping his head slightly, and brushed her lips with his. She forgot to breathe.

His lips were warm, firm, everything she remembered and so much that she'd forgotten. It was a short kiss, but it made her want more. So much more. Made her want to cry over the frustrating need that was pounding through her. It was as though there was a bottomless pit of need and desire in her, and she'd never known about it until now. Had never known it existed until Aleksei unearthed it.

She wobbled slightly when trying to step away from him, needing distance.

"I thought you were going to wait until I came to you," she said, not summoning up as much accusation in her voice as she'd have liked.

"I was," he said, dark humor lacing his voice, his accent seeming heavier. "But it was only a kiss."

How was something *only* anything when it had the power to tilt your world off its axis?

He was so tempting. But her resolution to let go of the past didn't mean she was going to jump into bed with her boss. Especially when she'd already tried that tired old cliché five years ago.

This had *Bad Idea* written all over it. It had taken her years, professionally and otherwise, to get back to normal after her last disastrous relationship with a man. She hadn't been able to get a job for nearly a year, because the scandal had been related to her work. No one wanted to bring her into the company.

Ultimately, she'd ended up getting a job at a catering company, serving food from a line. No one had cared there. Or maybe they hadn't known. Her boss's wife at the time, the wife she'd been ignorant of, was a semi-famous men's catalog model and B-movie actress. That was one reason her unintended affair had been headline news.

It had been hard to start at the bottom, especially after she'd graduated with such high honors, achieved a coveted, but ill-fated, internship. But at least at the bottom, in a new industry, away from the corporate setting, she'd been free from the ugliness.

But if she started a relationship with Aleksei…too stupid. It would be too stupid.

"Well, don't kiss me again. We're shooting for professional here, and that isn't it."

"Is it because I'm your boss, Madeline? Is that why you don't want this?"

"Partly," she said.

"And the other part?"

"Not your business, because you're my boss and not my lover."

"I'm not opposed to becoming your lover."

She looked at a spot on the wall behind him. She couldn't handle looking at him, not when he was offering her something she was fighting against wanting so desperately. Not when she knew one look in those midnight eyes would undo her completely.

"I know," she said. "But I work for you. That gives you… The power balance isn't fair. There's no way…I would be at a total disadvantage."

"That isn't how I operate. If we were to have an affair—" she cringed at his use of the word "—then I would be your boss during business hours, and your lover when we weren't at the office. As your lover, I wouldn't be your boss."

"And as my boss you wouldn't be my lover?"

"I already told you, I don't mix business with pleasure."

"I think *I* said that. And I also think it might mean something different than colleagues at work, lovers off work."

He shrugged. That he could even make such a casual gesture when she was ready to melt was infuriating. "If it were about a relationship, then, yes, I can see how it would be problematic to separate the two. But I'm not looking for a relationship."

"So, you just want...sex?"

He flexed the fingers on his left hand. "Exactly. I don't do relationships."

Most women would have been upset by that, and she realized that. Even understood why. She'd been one of those women. One who thought sex and love had to go together. Well, she'd been an idiot then.

Now she was relieved. He hadn't lied. He hadn't said he wanted to be with her because she was special. He hadn't said he loved her. He'd said he wanted sex. It was honest, at least.

Those other words...those were lies. Lies men told to make women feel comfortable. To make them feel indebted to them. *Oh, you love me so I owe you my body.*

What a sick joke that was.

"Well, I don't do the relationship thing either," she said, confident in that, if nothing else.

"So we're on the same page."

She laughed, a little hysterical bubble of sound escaping her lips. "I'll bet it's nearly impossible for the two of us to be on the same page."

"You want me," he said. Not a question.

"Yes." There was no point in lying. None at all.

"I want you. Seems like we might be on the same page."

His dark eyes were molten heat, intense, his expression hard and unmoving. He didn't try to coddle her, caress her, seduce her. He didn't add sweet words or a cajoling smile. He didn't try to relax her. Didn't offer her a drink to help calm her nerves.

Her heart was pounding so loud she was certain he could hear it. She knew what was smart. And she knew what she wanted. It was too bad they weren't the same thing.

She took a step toward him, and she knew. Knew that in doing that, she was saying yes.

And then his mouth was on hers, his lips and tongue urgent, his body hot and hard against hers. She moved against him, feeling the hard ridge of his erection against her stomach. She felt an answering wetness between her thighs, her breasts heavy, needing his touch.

Yes.

This was honest. His response couldn't be faked or concealed. He didn't try to make it into more than it was by lighting candles and draping a red scarf over a lamp. This wasn't some carefully plotted seduction. It was need. Beyond anything she'd felt before. It wasn't about emotion, or love, or wanting something, someone, to fill the void inside of her heart.

It wasn't about escape. It wasn't about the future. It was now and it was real. And it was the only thing that mattered.

The masculine growl that escaped his lips as he teased her with his moist tongue was a sound of pure, sexual desire. And that was what she wanted. All she wanted.

Physical, she could do. And she wanted physical with Aleksei. Yes, he was her boss, but there was nothing, nothing about him, that bore any resemblance to William Callahan.

There were no lies between she and Aleksei. No promises either.

Nothing but desire.

She'd thought, been afraid, that being with a man again would put her back in that vulnerable, needy place. Well, she was needy, but not in the way she'd been scared she would be. She was only needy for his touch. For the feeling of his hard body inside of hers.

But she also felt powerful. Felt like she had control. He was so hard against her there was no denying that he was on fire for her too, that he wanted what she did. That she was an equal partner.

She ran her hands over his chest. He was built like a fantasy come to life. Hard, well-defined muscles, broad shoulders. And right now, he was hers to explore. And she wanted to embark on the journey so badly she was shaking with her desire.

Excitement surged through her. She worked the buttons on the front of his shirt and pushed it down his arms, growling in frustration when the buttoned cuffs caught on his wrists. He chuckled and wrenched his mouth from hers, taking a moment to undo the buttons before shrugging his shirt off and letting it fall to the floor.

She swallowed hard when she saw his bare chest. He

looked better than he felt. Olive skin, perfectly defined, just the right amount of dark chest hair scattered over his pecs and continuing in a line down his abs until it disappeared beneath the waistband of his dark trousers.

He looked at her, his eyes appraising. He was too calm. She needed him out of control.

She approached him and put her hands on his belt, working the leather through the silver buckle before undoing the button on his pants. She kept her eyes trained on his. His jaw was clenched tight, muscles bunched.

Sucking in a sharp breath, she pressed her hand flat against his shaft, feeling the length of him. He was big. And it had been a long time. Briefly, she worried it might hurt. Her first time had been hellish that way, but then, she hadn't really been all that aroused at the time. She'd simply been eager to please. None of that had been about her.

Well, she was aroused now, beyond aroused. And this *was* about her. About taking something back that belonged to her. Her body. Her desire. Her right to want a man, and to act on that wanting.

Hooking her fingers in the waistband of his pants and underwear, she slid them down his slim hips, revealing his whole body to her. Naked, fully aroused, he was the most incredible sight she'd ever seen.

He was also a little bit intimidating.

"I haven't…been with anyone in a while," she said, looking at his fully aroused body.

"Then I'll make sure you're ready," he said.

And just like that her nerves, what little there had been, were taken care of. He would know what to do with a woman. She trusted that. Because Aleksei was a perfectionist, and he would make this perfect too.

"Now you," he said, putting his hands on the front of her blouse.

She batted them away, replacing them with her own hands. She undid the first button, the second, the third, gratified by the hunger she saw etched into his sculpted face. She let her shirt join his on the floor before shimmying out of her pencil skirt. Then she was standing before him in nothing more than stockings, high heels and a very sheer lace bra and panty set.

And she saw his control snap, the light in his eyes turning feral, just before all of the tension in his body released and he pulled her into his arms.

He moved his hands from her hips, to her waist, up to the catch of her bra. He flicked it open with one deft motion and the lacy garment fell away. She wasn't embarrassed for him to see her, not when it was obvious just how very much he was enjoying the sight.

Those magic hands shifted slightly, his thumbs skimming her ribcage, brushing against the swell of her breasts. Her nipples tightened, almost painfully. Why didn't he touch her there? She was dying for it. Needed it more than she needed air.

Aleksei didn't look away from her face, his dark eyes trained on hers. He didn't reach straight for her breasts, didn't grope or grab at her. Ironically, she wished he would.

He only continued stroking her skin in maddening circles before encircling her waist with his arms and drawing her up against his hard body.

He kissed her thoroughly, deeply, sensually, his tongue making thorough sweeps of her mouth. Her body shook, and she arched into him, her nipples brushing against his crisp chest hair. A moan of pleasure escaped her lips.

She didn't remember it being like this. She *knew* it hadn't been like this before. This was…everything she was feeling, all of the pleasure, the aching hollow need in her body, it was almost too much. In the very best way.

She moved against him, needing to stimulate the part of her body that was screaming loudest for his touch.

His hand moved from her hip down to her thigh, the sensual slide pure torture in the best sense. Gripping her leg, he drew it up around his, opening her to him, bringing her clitoris up against his hardened shaft.

"Yes," she whispered into his mouth, moving against him, taking everything that she craved.

"Yes," he answered, backing her up until her legs hit the desk.

Lifting her gently, he seated her on the polished surface. When he abandoned her lips, she felt dizzy, dazed. More than a little lightheaded.

Aleksei knelt in front of her and slid his hands beneath her panties, drawing them down her stocking-clad legs, delicately removing them and casting them onto the floor. She was open to him now, exposed. And she still wasn't embarrassed or ashamed.

There was no room for that. Not now.

That filled her with a different kind of exhilaration, one that was quickly overshadowed when he traced a line on her inner thigh with the tip of his tongue. She gritted her teeth. Oh, she had never felt anything like this before. Never experienced a rush of pleasure so divine. Her head fell back and she gripped the edge of the desk, hoping she didn't fall.

Rough, masculine hands moved to grip her thighs, to keep her from scooting away from him as he ran the flat of his tongue over that most sensitive part of her. She arched, tightening her hold on the edge of the desk. This was even better. Even more incredible.

Never, ever had she experienced this before. She'd thought about it, dabbled in the odd fantasy about what it might be like, knew it had to be amazing…but she'd underestimated.

Oh, she'd had no idea.

Aleksei's tongue was expert, and when he slid a finger into her tight passage she nearly flew into a million pieces. The addition of a second digit left her quivering, shaking, close to falling over the precipice she felt like she was on the edge of.

He was merciless, his tongue and fingers moving in time until she was pushed over the edge into oblivion. She let go of the edge of the desk and gripped his shoulders, digging her fingernails into his back. She didn't care. He didn't seem to care.

So that was what all the fuss was about.

She felt weak. Spent. But still somehow unsatisfied. And she knew why. She still hadn't had him inside of her. And it seemed absolutely critical for her to experience that.

"Can you stand up?" he asked, voice husky.

She nodded and stood from the desk. His hands were gentle, but firm, as he turned her so she was facing the desk and pressed slightly on her back. She put her hands flat on the polished surface. She'd never had sex in this position, but she was educated enough on the subject to know what he wanted.

A shiver of excitement ran through her.

She heard the sound of plastic tearing.

"Condom," he said.

A rush of relief flooded her, because she would have forgotten. She'd been too caught up in the moment. She still was. It was hard for her to think clearly, not with the buzz of her first orgasm still lingering, and raging arousal still roaring through her.

The blunt head of his erection probed at her slick entrance and she parted her legs further, trying to make sure she could accommodate him. He thrust into her slowly, painlessly, and she was grateful for that.

Then he gripped her hips and began to move. His rhythm hard, steady, intoxicating. He reached his hand around to the front of her body and cupped her breast, squeezing her nipple lightly. She didn't bother to hold back the moan that climbed her throat, didn't bother to disguise any of her reactions to the pleasure that was rocketing through her.

His hand moved to her clitoris, working in time with his thrusts. She grasped the edge of the desk again, needing something to hold her to earth as another climax started to build.

When it hit her, this time he was with her, his grunt of completion mingling with hers. He placed his hand, palm down, next to hers, resting his head against her shoulder, his breathing ragged, his heart raging.

"I have to move," she said, her knees too weak to support her.

He pulled back, out, and she collapsed into the nearest chair. Her head was spinning, her heart beating on overdrive.

She'd had sex. She'd enjoyed it. The roof hadn't caved

in. No one had come in and shouted and called her a whore.

It had even been her boss.

There was no media.

There was no guilt.

For the first time in five years, her body felt like it belonged to her again. Everything, for so long, had been tied up in the man who had stolen what was left of her innocence. Had taken the last shred of her belief in humanity and used it against her.

And because of him she'd locked her desires away, felt guilty for even looking twice at a man, because she felt she couldn't even trust her own body.

Not only had all of that been erased, she'd learned that there really was a lot more to sex than she knew. And she was glad for that. Her few experiences with William had left her disappointed.

She'd wanted so desperately to please him, to be the woman for him. To be worthy of his love.

Tonight, she'd pleased herself. And her lover looked pretty pleased too.

Aleksei turned away from her, discreetly discarding the condom in a wastebasket before picking his pants up from the floor and jerking them on in one fast motion.

She couldn't move yet. She could only look at her clothes, scattered all over the office floor, and wonder what exactly she'd been transformed into in Aleksei's arms.

She looked down and realized she was still wearing her stay-up nylons and high heeled shoes. What a picture she must make. She waited, again, for the guilt.

The shame. Nothing. She simply felt…satisfied. Very, very satisfied.

"I…" she said, searching for words.

"It wasn't a good idea?" he asked, buckling his belt.

"No, it really wasn't. But it's too late now."

"It was too late the moment we saw each other," he said, a wry smile on his lips.

"I think you're probably right." She scooted the chair forward and reached down, scooping up her bra and panties. "I don't regret it."

"Good," he said. "Because it's a little late for regrets."

"But it was just sex," she said.

"Yes."

She sighed. "Good sex."

He grunted in agreement as he tugged his shirt on.

"And it shouldn't happen again," she finished.

His movements stilled. "Oh, no?"

"No. We have to work together and now that we've… well, we've got it out of our systems it would be best to go back to work."

One dark eyebrow lifted. "If that's what you want."

"It is." It had to be. It had been amazing and at the moment she felt wonderfully, blessedly detached. She wasn't risking that detachment.

Of course, Aleksei had never promised love. Never promised a ring and a house and a family and everything she'd ever wanted.

She didn't want those things now anyway. They were an illusion. Love was only a mask for control. She didn't believe in it now, didn't want it.

"Yeah, I think…it has to be over now."

He nodded. "I'll let you dress." He turned to walk out of the office, then paused. "I need you to come to the studio tomorrow. I have some things I need to show you so that we can come to a consensus on displays."

"Okay," she said, still feeling unshakeable, unbreakable, in the aftermath of her new experience.

"See you tomorrow." Then he left. And she was alone.

And suddenly she felt very, very alone.

She cursed into the empty room and began to gather her clothes.

CHAPTER SEVEN

It HAD been twelve hours since he'd been inside of Madeline's body. Twelve hours and his body was still infused with a rush of post-orgasm adrenaline. She had been incredible. Gorgeous, eager, uninhibited.

And she only wanted the one time.

Usually, the promise of one time would settle well with him. He wasn't looking for commitment, not even close. But another taste of the sweet oblivion being lost in Madeline's body afforded? That he would gladly experience again.

He glanced at his watch right when Madeline came bursting through the door of his studio.

"You're late," he said, taking a long moment to admire her beauty.

Her cheeks were flushed from the outside air, and from the run it looked like she'd taken to try and make it on time. Long, slender legs encased in dark, skinny jeans that hugged her hips. A stretchy cotton top with a scoop neckline that molded to her rounded breasts. Breasts he'd had in his hands twelve hours ago.

He hadn't taken the time to taste them, and now he regretted that.

"Sorry...I overslept." She looked down when she said it.

"Didn't sleep well last night?" He certainly hadn't. His body had been hard and aching for round two.

He'd forgotten how good sex was, as strange as it was to admit. Had forgotten the bliss of having nothing on his mind but his own pleasure and the pleasure of his partner. Now he was craving more. More of Madeline.

"Come back this way," he said.

The studio was empty. Most of his designers opted to come in, borrow specific tools, and work from home. It was better that way. Too many artistic egos in one room quickly became chaotic.

He opened the door to his workroom, a room he hadn't been in in maybe two years before these past few weeks, and ushered her inside.

"Do you have the necklace here?"

The note of excitement in her voice was strangely gratifying. "In the safe."

He pressed his thumbprint to a pad in the wall, then keyed in a code that opened his personal safe. There was no such thing as being too careful when jewelry of the quality he worked with was involved.

He took out a velvet box and opened it, watching Madeline's eyes carefully. They widened, obvious approval evident in them. "It's so beautiful, Aleksei."

She reached out, delicate fingers hovering over the gems.

"Touch it if you like," he said, aware his voice sounded rough.

Her eyes met his and she lowered her fingers, caressing the emeralds in a reverent manner. One that made his blood pound hot and fast. He wanted her hands on him again.

Last time had been hot and fast. Incredible. But he wanted more time. Time to savor her body, to thoroughly enjoy every inch of her lovely curves. Desk sex in his office had been amazing, hot, wild, but a soft bed was the preferred venue for good reasons.

"Try it on," he said.

Her blue eyes flew to his. "Why?"

"I want to see it. I have never put it on anyone before. Which means I have never really seen it."

She hesitated, her hand hovering over the box. "I…"

"Let me." He set the box on the desk and lifted the necklace from its satin casing. "Turn around," he said, the echo from the day before sending all of his blood south, making him painfully hard.

It was easy to see her in his mind as she'd been then. Her body stretched over the desk, the elegant line of her back, the indent of her small waist. The curve of her hip, her perfectly round butt. And those long legs, long even though she was petite, with those black stockings still on.

She looked up at him and licked her lips, a glitter of wariness in her eyes. But she obeyed, turning slowly so that she was facing away from him. He lifted the necklace from its case and swept her thick curtain of dark hair aside, his thumb brushing the creamy, smooth skin of her neck.

He'd had sex with her. The mystery should be solved, all questions answered. And yet so many lingered. Her reaction to the first climax he'd given her…it had been explosive, but more than that, she'd seemed shell-shocked. He wanted to know why. Wanted to know why it had been a while since she'd been with anyone.

Mostly, he wanted to know what her pretty pink nipples tasted like.

He looped the necklace around with one hand, fastening it in the back and letting the heavy weight of it rest on her chest.

"Let me see," he said.

He gripped her shoulders and turned her slowly. It wasn't a line, what he'd said about seeing jewelry on a woman, it was the truth. He never really felt he'd seen a piece until it was being worn.

On Madeline, the necklace was exquisite. Large emeralds and small pear-cut diamonds woven together in a platinum chain. Some of the glittering diamonds dropped to the curve of her breasts, demanding that he look at her ripe, tempting flesh.

"You should wear it," he said.

She touched the lowest hanging diamond, the one that was nearly nestled in the valley of her cleavage. "I *am* wearing it."

"To the exhibition in Luxembourg. It is best displayed on you."

She opened her mouth and he could tell, by the stubborn set of those pretty lips, that she was about to argue.

"Madeline," he said, "don't say anything about professional boundaries. Because those were well and truly breached last night."

Her cheeks turned a deep crimson. "It happened. It isn't happening again, so professional boundaries do matter."

The desire to kiss her, touch her, caress her where those tiny diamonds glittered, was nearly impossible to combat. That by itself gave him the willpower to move away. Anything, any feeling, that was that strong…

It was simply unsatisfied desire. That was all. He'd had his taste, and now he wanted to eat his fill. His reaction was simply that of a hungry man in need of satiation.

Need. It was a word he didn't like. He'd needed someone before, and he had no intention of ever needing anyone again. And that meant he was going to have to deny the arousal that was coursing in his veins.

He could find a blonde. Or a redhead. Variety was always good. And he could go back to the carefully, controlled form of relationships he preferred. The sort of relationships that didn't include spontaneous sex on a desk.

It was better that way.

"I still want you to wear it," he said.

"You could hire a model," she retorted.

"But it looks perfect on you. Why should I pay some skinny woman to walk around in it when it suits you?"

Blue eyes narrowed in his direction. "Did you just imply that I'm fat?"

"No, I implied that professional models are skinny. You have curves. You are a woman." Curves that had fit in his hands perfectly, curves he was longing to touch again.

"Women want to be skinny, Aleksei. Good grief, I thought you were some sort of legendary playboy. Seems like you should know that."

Madeline wasn't really annoyed with Aleksei. Well, not about the skinny comment. She was annoyed at herself. Because the minute she'd walked into the room her sophisticated, blasé self, the one that had got dressed this morning repeating the mantra, "I can have a one-night stand and then face the man the next day, because I'm totally sure in myself," had gone and run for cover, leaving her nervous, and breathless, and a little turned on. Okay, a lot turned on.

And when he'd commanded her to turn around in that same tone as he'd used yesterday… It had melted her. Physically, not emotionally.

It had felt… It had been strange to have him leave after they'd been together. But ultimately, she was glad he had. No point in cuddling up. That was part of *making love*. They had not made love on that desk. That had been nothing but purely physical sex.

And the purely physical part of herself wanted him. A lot. Again. Maybe a couple more agains after that. But she hadn't known that sex could be *so* good.

She'd done the whole crying after, emotional thing before. But she'd never done the pleasure-that-felt-like-it-might-kill-you thing before. And she liked it. Which brought her back to the wanting more thing. Which was really impractical and not going to happen.

But was kind of hard with Aleksei's dark gaze trained on her, his eyes full of heat and, she was sure she saw it, desire.

"I didn't find the statement insulting," he said. "I like your figure."

"Boundaries," she said, not as sharply as she would have liked.

"You like me to cross boundaries."

She thought he might kiss her. But he didn't. He only looked at her. But that look had the power to melt the soles of her shoes. She waited for him to make a move. He didn't.

The disappointment that settled in her stomach irritated her. She shouldn't be disappointed. She was the one who'd said it was one time only. For very good reasons. Aleksei, or rather Aleksei's bedroom skills, were addictive. And whether she was with him one time or ten, they always would be. So there was no point in prolonging it, in making it more important than it needed to be.

More important than it could be.

There was no room in her life for emotional entanglements. And she didn't even believe that love really existed. Her brother and his wife were extremely happy, even after five years. But of course some people were compatible, so it was bound to work.

She'd never seen real love up close in action. Her parents certainly hadn't loved anyone but themselves. Definitely not their unexpected, unwanted daughter. William hadn't loved her. All of his compliments, all of his poetic words, had been designed to manipulate her into bed. Had been to make her docile and happy so she didn't ask why he didn't stay the night, and why they never went to his house. And why it was a secret they were together.

She'd been so stupid.

She never would be again. At least with Aleksei it was just the sex and she knew it.

"I can't deny that I liked it," she said.

Oh, good, and now her cheeks were hot, which meant they were bright pink with embarrassment. She just wasn't a sexually sophisticated person, and one time with Aleksei hadn't changed that.

"But," she continued, "that doesn't change the fact

that it was a bad idea, and…and we have to get back to business now."

"I fail to see what any of this has to do with you wearing the necklace. Even if yesterday hadn't happened, now I've seen you in the necklace, you're the one I would want displaying it."

Okay, this was work. It was just work. She was good at this. Besides, the necklace was gorgeous. She admired what Aleksei did so much, saw so much art and beauty in it. She was really almost honored to be asked to wear it.

"As part of my job?" she asked.

"As part of your job."

She nodded slowly. "Okay. I'll wear it."

Because he was her boss, and he was asking her to. But it felt different…and that was because they'd…been together.

All the more reason to just wear the necklace. If she let a few stolen moments of pleasure, the kind of pleasure she'd denied herself for so long, the kind of pleasure she deserved, ruin her job, then she'd have sabotaged her career for sex. And that was even stupider than sleeping with her boss had been in the first place.

"If you need a gown, I will have one purchased for you," he said.

"You sign my paychecks, Aleksei, you know I can afford a gown if I need one," she answered tightly.

"It's for a company event. Shouldn't the company provide it for you?"

She chewed her lip. "Maybe, under normal circumstances."

He shrugged and raised his dark eyebrows. "I thought circumstances were normal."

Maddy made an exasperated sound in the back of her throat. "They are. But they aren't. If you bought me a gown, when you never have before, given what happened, it would make me feel cheap."

"That would not be my intent."

Her stomach tightened. She didn't suppose it was usually a man's intent to make a woman feel cheap. Just like he wasn't lavishing her with attention when all he was really giving her was things.

She'd liked the things William had bought for her. She'd imagined them to be thoughtful. A sign he was thinking of her. Her parents had never bothered to buy her anything, and they didn't care about her at all, so maybe...

Grrrr. She refocused her thoughts. She wasn't going there. She wasn't doing the self-pity thing. The long and the short of it was that taking a gift from Aleksei, at this point, wasn't happening.

"You know why it wouldn't be appropriate," she said, meeting his eyes, feeling the impact down to her toes and at all the interesting points in between.

"You're being ridiculous, Madeline."

"No," she said. "No, I'm not. You're in the position of ultimate power, so you don't get it. I know what it's like to be the one dependent on someone for something. To be the one at a disadvantage. Yesterday happened, and while it isn't happening again, it doesn't change the fact that it did, and that it alters the dynamic between us. I'm not going to let you...buy me, so just let me buy my own dress."

"What's this about, Madeline? Because I'm sure it has nothing to do with me specifically. When have I ever acted like I owned you? Or like I even wanted to?"

"Let's just not talk about it," she said, clipped.

"Fine with me. But I'm buying your dress."

"No, Aleksei…"

"Madeline, last I checked, I was your boss. As you so eloquently reminded me a moment ago, I sign your paychecks. The fact that I had sex with you doesn't mean you can suddenly disagree with everything I say."

"I want to choose it," she said.

"Fine, I trust your judgment as far as fashion is concerned."

Maddy rubbed her forehead, trying to ease the tension there. "Well, that's something."

"I'll have to approve it of course."

"Oh, for heaven's sake, Aleksei!" she hissed. There would be no easing the tension in her head now.

"It's my display, for my jewelry."

"Your *display* is *my* body."

"I will not force you to wear something you're uncomfortable with. I simply want to ensure I'm happy with how it complements the necklace."

She sucked in a sharp breath. Things had got out of hand, and all because of yesterday. She'd been congratulating herself on how emotionless it had been, and now she was feeling extra touchy about everything.

"Okay, fine. I'll buy a few dresses I like and I'll show them to you and return the ones you don't like, fair?" she asked.

"Fair enough," said Aleksei.

He touched her shoulder, his fingers rough from the fine work he did with his hands, his palm hot. Then he reached around with his other hand and unclasped the necklace, sliding it off of her, the cool metal a sharp contrast to his touch.

How was it possible to be so annoyed at a man and to want him so much at the same time? Maybe that was how it worked when there was no love involved. If desire was divorced from emotion it didn't really matter how she felt about Aleksei. It only mattered that she was still attracted to him.

It made everything inside of her a strange series of compartments. Aleksei her boss, Aleksei the man she'd slept with, Aleksei the man who sometimes drove her crazy.

As long as she was able to keep it all separate, everything would be fine. And she would. Because she had no other choice.

It had been two weeks since Aleksei had been inside Madeline's body. Two weeks since he'd touched her, tasted her. And it was a sad commentary on the power of his attraction to her that he remembered the exact date he'd been with her.

He hadn't found another woman. He'd considered it. Had even considered calling Olivia for a brief and satisfying reconciliation. But he hadn't. Because it wouldn't be satisfying. Not in the way it had been to be with Madeline.

He wanted more of her, and until he had it he could not see wanting anyone else.

He had been working in the Milan office more. It was more convenient at the moment because of the upcoming exhibition in Luxembourg. It was also a form of sexual torture he found almost intriguing. To see Madeline and not have her. To want something he couldn't have. To actually want anything and anyone specifically. It was all fascinating in a way.

He hadn't desired a certain woman in a long time. It had been more about a need for sex than for anyone in particular. But Madeline…he desired her. Likely because she had ended things before their natural conclusion. Because she had ended things, period. He couldn't remember if a woman had ever ended things with him before. It was always his call to end the relationship.

The intercom on his phone beeped, and his secretary's voice came over the speaker. "Madeline Forrester is here to see you. She says she has the dresses."

A slight chuckle rose in his throat. "Send her in."

Thirty seconds later the door to his office opened and Madeline strode in, three garment bags draped over her arm, her long brown hair loose around her shoulders.

"I come bearing gowns," she said.

He hadn't seen her very often over the course of the past couple weeks. Brief meetings in her office, and he'd passed her a few times walking through the vast lobby of the office building. Every time she was polite, but seemingly unaffected.

Except for the flush of rose that stained her cheeks whenever she met his gaze.

She looked at him and her cheeks darkened. Satisfaction tightened his stomach. She still wanted him. But if she wanted him, it would be her who made the move. He was hardly going to chase after a woman, especially one doing such a good job of feigning disinterest.

She would have to admit it. Would have to acknowledge how much she wanted him.

She stepped forward and draped the bags over his desk. "So, I'll leave them for you to inspect and you can get back to me about which one you like."

He placed his hand over hers, catching it before she could pull it away from the bags. "No, that's not how this is going to work."

"Oh, no?" She lifted one well-shaped brow at him, the curve of her left hip cocked to the side in defiance.

"No. You must try them on for me."

Her mouth dropped open and she pulled that smooth, sexy hand away from him. "That's…objectifying."

"How? You're going to wear one of them in front of me anyway, and I assume all are entirely appropriate for public viewing."

She shut her mouth, her teeth clicking loudly. "True."

"Then what's the problem?"

That bottom lip of hers, so lush and kissable, got a very good chewing on as she decided what to say. He knew she wouldn't have much of anything to say ultimately. Because her issue with it pertained to their having sex with each other and he knew she'd rather chew glass than bring it up.

"Nothing," she said finally, releasing her lower lip.

"You can change in there." He gestured toward the bathroom that was at the far end of his office.

She scooped the garment bags back up in her arms and walked into the bathroom, shutting the door behind her. He had to laugh when he heard the unmistakable click of the lock. Then he had to acknowledge it was probably a good thing she'd locked it, or he might be tempted to go in and help her with zippers or something.

And then he'd end up stripping her bare and having his way with her on the vanity.

His body pulsed in serious approval of that fantasy. He let it play in his mind for a while, much longer than he usually allowed himself, until Madeline came out of

the bathroom, perfect curves encased in a long emer-
ald-green gown. It was strapless, but the cut was high
and didn't reveal enough of her gorgeous breasts for his
taste.

Though, staying on task, the real issue was that he
wanted to see the effect of the necklace on her skin and
not on heavy green satin.

"Next," he said.

She shot him a deadly glare. "I like this one."

"Keep it then, but don't wear it with my necklace."

Lifting the skirt and kicking it to one side, she saun-
tered back into the bathroom. She was sexy, even when
she was in a snit. Perhaps especially then. He liked her
spirit, liked the fact that she wasn't afraid to have a little
verbal battle with him. Women, people in general, usually deferred to him. Even Paulina had looked to him
for answers, had waited on his approval.

Not Madeline.

She reappeared a few moments later in a black dress
that was fitted all the way until it hit her knees, then
billowed out with flowing fabric. The neckline plunged
to her sternum, the pale skin on display so tempting it
was all he could do to remain at his desk.

The necklace would make the dress more modest,
would show hints of those glorious breasts without revealing too much. It would be perfect.

"That's it," he said.

He stood and walked across the room, coming to
look more closely. Because he had to.

"I have one more," she said, taking a step back.

"This is it," he repeated.

She quirked her mouth to one side and put a hand on
her hip. "Ta-da."

He felt his lips lift into a smile. "Turn for me."

She shot him a glare but turned slowly. The dress hugged that tight rear end of hers that he was so fond of, showed the tiny dip of her waist. Yes, it was the perfect dress. All eyes would be on her with or without the necklace.

She looked up at him and he felt the impact of her gorgeous blue eyes streak through him. He could remember the last time she'd looked at him like that, her color high in her cheeks, her breasts rising and falling with her rapid breathing.

The last time she'd looked at him like that he'd ended up taking her over his desk.

He could hear the sounds of employees milling around in the next room. Stripping that dress off Madeline's gorgeous body and having his way with her now would be incredibly stupid. Although, even knowing that, it was very tempting.

His teeth ached. He wanted her so badly. He honestly couldn't recall the last time sex had held such power over him. He was thirty-three years old. He'd been in love, been married, had lost his wife. He'd lived a full lifetime by the time he was twenty-seven. With all of that experience behind him, he was a difficult man to captivate.

And yet he felt captivated.

He couldn't understand what it was about this one woman that appealed to him so. Couldn't understand why she brought out desires that had been buried for so long. But he didn't want love from Madeline. He wanted sex. He wanted satisfaction. And that day, she had wanted the same.

She wanted the same now. He could see it written all

over her beautiful face. Could see that her entire body was taut with the effort it took for her to hold herself back, to keep from reaching out and touching him.

Her need mirrored his own. And the last time they had given in, it had been explosive. He wanted to give in again. He wasn't a man given to vices. He wasn't a man who gave in to temptation.

But he was considering the benefits of becoming that man.

"You look beautiful, Madeline."

She sucked in a sharp breath, the hollows in her neck deepening. "I don't need to hear that from you, Aleksei."

"Because I'm your boss?"

"Because I dislike it when men use compliments to try and seduce me."

"Happen often?"

She narrowed her eyes. "A couple times that I can think of. I much preferred it when you said you wanted sex, without trying to cushion it with flattery. That was honest, at least."

"So is this. You are beautiful, Madeline, and it has to be said. Even if I never touch you again, I had to say it."

Her breathing increased and she blinked rapidly. He thought he might have seen tears in her eyes. But as quickly as they had appeared, they were gone. No, his prickly Madeline wouldn't cry in front of him.

When had he started thinking of her as his?

"Just...don't, Aleksei, please," she whispered.

Seeing Madeline vulnerable did strange things to him. It made him feel...responsible. It made him *feel*.

"You don't think you're beautiful, Madeline?" he asked.

"It doesn't matter what I think. I just don't trade compliments and lies for sex."

"That wasn't my goal. If I decide to seduce you, you'll know exactly what I'm doing. I would kiss you again, press you back against my desk. I would never lie to get you into bed. I think we've both proven that I don't have to."

She turned red, from the base of her neck to her cheeks. "True," she bit out.

"That's one thing you can count on from me, Madeline. Honesty. As your boss, and as a lover."

She swallowed. "I want to believe that."

"I don't say things I don't mean, and I don't manipulate to get what I want."

"Then…thank you. For saying I'm beautiful." She edged away from him before turning and making her way back to the bathroom and closing the door behind her.

He noticed, after she'd left, that she hadn't promised him honesty in return.

CHAPTER EIGHT

"How is it looking over there, Madeline?"

That voice. That voice that haunted her dreams. Issuing rough, explicit commands, and, more disturbingly, sweet, soft words. That voice that she heard every day on the other end of the phone issuing work-related commands.

Why did his voice have to make her nipples hard and her body ache for him to be inside of her again?

The why didn't really matter. It was that it did, that was the problem. It had been over a month since she'd last touched Aleksei. Two weeks since she'd seen him, since he'd returned to Moscow to take care of some work there.

And she still wanted him.

"Everything looks great, Aleksei," she said, burrowing under the plush covers.

She was at the castle in Luxembourg, preparing everything for the exhibition that was taking place in four days, and she was very fortunate to be staying in one of the castle's many fabulous guestrooms.

It was all very medieval, but with every modern convenience imaginable. It also catered to some latent princess fantasies Maddy hadn't been aware she'd been harboring. But the four-poster bed, complete with gauzy swaths of fabric and lavish bedding, was certainly fit for a princess. And, for now, she was owning it.

Getting the ballroom sorted out had been a big project and she was in bed early in anticipation of working on the smaller displays for the other rooms bright and way too early in the morning.

"And you have the team climbing ladders for you?" he asked, his rich voice sending a little shiver through her.

She squirmed beneath the heavy comforter, wishing that she was still dressed in her work clothes and not in bed in a silky nightgown that barely covered the tops of her thighs.

"I promise my Manolos haven't so much as touched a ladder rung."

"Good."

She shifted and tugged her covers up higher. "What about you, Mr. Petrov? Are you still at the office, burning the midnight oil? Burning the candle at both ends? Burning out?"

"Very nice, Madeline," he said, the humor that laced his voice unexpected, making pleasure curl in her stomach. "And, no, as it happens. I'm at home. In bed."

Her heart lurched and she tightened her grip on the phone. "Really?"

"Yes. Even I have to sleep sometimes."

It was strange to think of Aleksei as a mere mortal. Not when there were so many times he seemed like a lot more than that. "Nice to get…comfy and in your pajamas, I guess."

He chuckled, a sound that made her already tight nipples burn. "I don't wear pajamas."

Her heart hammered hard and her breath was coming short and harsh. And before she could censor herself or think anything through, she asked him the next question that came to her mind.

"So that means you're wearing nothing, I suppose?" Her left hand was curled into a tight fist, gripping a chunk of her thick, down-filled comforter.

"Nothing at all," he responded, his accent thicker, his voice deeper, huskier.

A muffled moan escaped her lips and he chuckled again.

"Madeline, what are you thinking?" he asked.

About pleasure. About the way he had looked, naked and unashamed in his office. About hot, wonderful sex like she'd never known existed before she'd met him.

"About you," she said, her words rushed. "About your body."

There was a slight pause. When Aleksei spoke his voice was rough, strained.

"What about you, Madeline? Do you wear pajamas?"

She bit her lips and brushed a hand over her silky nightgown. Did she continue the game? Or let it end?

Her heart was pounding hard, her body aching. Just a little more.

"I'm wearing a nightgown. It's really silky and short. Pink."

"Perfect. But I think I would like you better without it."

Oh, things were getting out of hand. She shifted beneath the thick comforter, her hand still clinging to it as if it was her lifeline. A link to her sanity. Never mind that it was failing. Never mind that she couldn't think of anything when Aleksei spoke but naked limbs tangled together and the desire for that deep satisfaction only he had ever given her.

It was too easy to imagine him in bed beside her, him without pajamas, his hand exploring the skin beneath her barely-there nightie.

She wanted him to keep talking. Wanted to ask him if he was hard. If he was as turned on as she was. Her throat was completely dry and her palms were slick with sweat. Her hands were shaking now with desire, nerves and a healthy shot of adrenaline.

She wanted him. She wanted him so much she could barely breathe. It was crazy. Ridiculous. Stupid.

What was she doing? Oh, heaven help her, what was she doing?

"I should go," she choked out.

There was a long pause. The tension nearly killed her. Would he say more? Would he ask her if she was aroused? If she wanted him? And if he did, would she have the strength to hang up?

"Goodnight, Madeline."

Disappointment and relief flooded her in equal measures. Her throat was so tight she couldn't speak. She snapped the phone shut without saying goodbye and buried her face in her pillow. Not even the phone was safe anymore. She couldn't talk to Aleksei, couldn't think about him, and she certainly couldn't share a room with him, without wanting to have a reenactment of those hot, heady moments in his office.

Why not?

They weren't getting back to normal. She'd practically subjected him to a heavy breathing call just now. There was nothing professional about that. She'd had sex with him once already. And nothing dramatic or horrible had happened. She wasn't in love.

Why not do it again? Why not let it run its course?

A jolt shook her body at the thought. Could she do that? A no-strings fling? Well, she wasn't doing one-night stand very well, so why not try a brief fling?

More of Aleksei, his magic hands and lips and tongue. Her whole body heated at the thought. Then she shivered a little.

She was actually thinking of being a normal woman. Of chasing after what she desired. Of letting go of that horrible mistake she'd made that still controlled so much.

There, she was doing it. She was committed. There was no way to have her relationship with Aleksei be normal, so she might as well have it be what she wanted.

Now all she had to do was re-seduce her boss.

The entire ballroom of the castle had been made to look like a fairytale. The real world was totally absent from the fantasy Madeline and her team had spun from the gorgeous architecture. Glittering gems were displayed on velvet pillows, placed on pedestals.

The only thing that was missing was the gem of the hour. And the woman that was supposed to be wearing it.

Madeline had been noticeably scarce since Aleksei had arrived.

That phone call. Her breathy voice, the moan of desire she'd made when he'd confessed to not wearing anything…it had caused him more sleepless nights than were excusable for a grown man with his level of experience.

He had been so close to embarrassing himself, simply from the sound of her voice.

There were a lot of women at the exhibition. Beautiful women. He hardly saw any of them.

He tightened his hand into a fist and took a slow breath in. Madeline, his experience with her, it was so tied up in fantasy that he must be remembering it as more than it had been. No sex was that good. No woman had that kind of power.

His arms prickled and he looked up. Madeline was descending the wide marble staircase and entering the grand ballroom. Her hair was curled and captured in a ponytail that was fastened low and cascaded over one shoulder. Her eyes, her beautiful blue eyes, were enhanced with the perfect amount of makeup. And those lush lips were painted red.

He wanted to kiss every bit of that red off her lips. See them swollen and pink as they had been that night. He stood from his table and began to walk to her. Her eyes caught his and held. And she didn't turn away.

Heat churned in his stomach. Need. Desire. Lust.

And it was all reflected in her bold stare. Her tempting body was on display, but it was her eyes that held him captive. Her eyes that held the explicit invitation he wanted to accept.

She stopped in front of him and her tongue darted out, slicking over those red lips. "You were right about the dress," she said. "It looks perfect with the necklace." She touched one of the emeralds with her delicate fingers.

"And I was right about you being beautiful."

She looked down. "You don't need to say that."

He took her chin between his thumb and forefinger

and tilted her face up so she had to meet his eyes again. "I told you, Madeline. I always tell the truth."

Maddy took a deep breath and extended her hand, touching Aleksei's. "Dance with me?"

His dark gaze was hot and her body responded instantly. Yes, this was the right choice. Otherwise, their one time together would always live in the realm of fantasy. A few heady moments too incredible to be real. There would be no closure.

It needed to be put firmly in reality, rather than being this mythical moment forever frozen in time, and much more important than it needed to be.

It would always be important for one reason. It was the moment she'd chosen to take control back. But it was about her. Not him. And so was this.

Of course, that didn't mean it couldn't be mutually pleasurable. She fully intended it to be. Part of the rush of power and euphoria from last time had been seeing how she'd affected him.

"Are you asking me to dance as my employee?"

She took a step closer. "Hopefully as your lover." It took every ounce of her courage to meet his eyes as she said that, but she did. She wasn't going to be ashamed of her desire. If he said no, then he said no.

"Come," he said, gripping her hand and leading her to the dance floor.

He placed his hand low and flat on her back and drew her to him. She went willingly, wrapping her arms around his neck, exulting in his touch, his warmth, his scent. She'd missed him.

That realization sent a shock through her system before she shook it off. Of course she'd missed him. Even if the attraction between them wasn't based on love, it was natural for her to miss his touch. That was just the way it was between lovers.

A small smile tugged at the corners of her mouth and she rested her head on his chest.

"Madeline," he said, his voice vibrating against her cheek. "If you keep clinging to me like that I won't make it through the evening."

She lifted her head and drew back slightly. "Well, I worked too hard on all of this for you to miss it. Do you approve?"

He smiled down at her, just a slight curve of his lips. Aleksei didn't do full-blown grins. There was always reserve there. "It's perfect."

Suddenly, her heart felt too big for her chest. She cleared her throat. "Thank you."

She wanted to believe it. Wanted to believe him when he said she was beautiful too. But…it was hard. It was hard to stop looking for the ulterior motive.

He touched her face, brushed his thumb over her bottom lip before leaning in to drop a light kiss on her mouth. It wasn't hot, or hungry, or any of the other things kisses from Aleksei usually were. Of course, kisses from Aleksei tended to result in nudity and they were in a public place, so it was likely for the best.

He rubbed his nose against hers and she nearly melted. Then he pressed a kiss to her cheek, her jaw, the spot just below her ear.

"Oh, Aleksei, please. I won't last through the party if you keep doing that."

"I'm not seeing the downside to that."

"I'm selling the necklace, remember? And I'm supposed to circulate, and overhear conversations, and…"

"Somehow it's slipped my mind." He kissed the

curve of her neck and she felt goosebumps break out over her arms.

He pulled his head back and looked at her, his dark eyes unreadable. "What changed your mind, Madeline?"

"I just… Our relationship isn't going back to normal. Why add sexual frustration to the awkwardness?"

He laughed, the most genuine laugh she'd ever heard from him. It made her stomach flip. It was the strangest sensation, as though she could feel his amusement in her. She wasn't sure if she liked the feeling at all.

"That's a good point, I suppose," he said, not missing a beat. Not experiencing the same surreal thing she had just been experiencing.

"It's practical."

"Are you sexually frustrated?" he asked, and this time she could read his eyes. She could feel the heat.

"If I wasn't, I wouldn't have shortcircuited on the phone with you the other day."

"Is that what that was? A glitch in internal wiring?"

"Something like that. Or maybe just…well, it comes back to the sexual frustration."

"And you've decided to relieve that."

"I can't think of a better way." She moved her hands over the broad expanse of his shoulders. "Believe me, I tried."

"That does wonders for my ego."

"Your ego is fine."

"No thanks to you," he said. He nipped the tender skin of her neck and then soothed it with his tongue.

"Aleksei," she said, the warning she'd intended to inject into her tone noticeably absent.

"All right, maybe dancing is a bad idea."

"A very bad idea. But then, since when was any of

this a good idea?" She laughed, a nervous, unnatural sound.

Aleksei studied Madeline's face. Her color was high, eyes bright. She looked aroused and nervous and beautiful. And she was right. It wasn't a good idea. Looking at her...it made his heart beat faster. That his heart was affected at all was far too dangerous. She was a flame, and he was captivated, and even though he knew it was a bad idea, he wanted to reach out and touch her.

He couldn't turn her away. He wouldn't. There was no real danger to his heart. That was an illusion. His heart was too hard. The injuries he'd sustained had healed over and left scars too tough for anyone to penetrate. As he liked it. As he intended.

This was simply desire. Strong desire, consuming desire. But it was limited to lust, nothing more.

Aleksei was dimly aware of the fact that there were photographers near them, and that they were discreetly taking pictures. He was also dimly aware that it was a very good thing. That the photos would evoke romance and show the necklace Madeline was wearing to perfection. But he was only dimly aware of those things. Most of his body was consumed by the need to get across the ballroom and up to his suite as quickly as possible.

"I think the party's over for us," he said.

She met his gaze. He saw her confidence falter. Then she took a breath, tightened her hold on his shoulders. "I think you're right."

He took her hand and led her from the dance floor to the foot of the broad staircase. Madeline looked sideways at the paparazzi. They blended in pretty seamlessly, nothing like the gutter press that charged people in the street, but she still noticed them.

"I was thinking we could find a side entrance and… sneak out," she said.

"Oh, yes, that's kind of your thing, isn't it?"

"No, it's not," she said, "but there's press everywhere."

"All the more reason to make a visible exit. To show the necklace off." He touched the jewels at the base of her throat, his hand hot, sending liquid warmth rushing through her body.

The press. One of her very personal demons. And Aleksei wanted her to walk out, on his arm, her boss's arm, looking very much like they were headed upstairs to do exactly what they were headed upstairs to do.

So does fear still control everything? Or do you?

"I do," she said under her breath.

"Are you ready?"

She met Aleksei's dark gaze and her heart beat strong, steady. She knew what she was doing. She was doing exactly what she wanted, and she wasn't letting her fear win.

"I'm ready."

He put his hand low on her back as they ascended the stairs, and walked out of the ballroom. Aleksei stopped at the double doors and pressed a kiss to her cheek. She saw a camera flash out of the corner of her eye.

She did her best not to flinch.

He put his hand on the back of her neck and soothed the tension there as they walked out of the ballroom and into the expansive corridor. It was packed with people too, eating canapés and drinking champagne, clustered around the small jewelry displays and admiring the different pieces.

"You don't like the press?" he asked, his voice low as they wove through the crowd.

"Not at all," she said tightly.

They were stopped by several people, women who wanted pictures with him, and who wanted to examine the necklace Maddy was wearing. It really was a show-stopping piece. Of course, Aleksei was rather show-stopping himself, in Madeline's opinion.

And he was hers. For a while, he was going to be hers to explore, to pleasure… Her body tightened, ached, with need.

"Let's hurry," she whispered, when they escaped another group of gawkers.

"I knew I hired you for a reason."

The crowd thinned around the curved staircase that led to the guestrooms. Aleksei took her hand and led the way up the narrow passage and Maddy followed, breathless, laughing. Happy.

When was the last time she'd been happy? She worked. She had drive. She had goals and ambition. She was content. But happiness? She wasn't sure if she'd ever been truly happy. But she was now. She felt…free. For the first time in her life, the chains from her past, a past that went well beyond her disastrous affair with William, didn't seem to be holding her down.

"My room is this way." Aleksei gestured to another staircase at the center of a long hallway.

"You have a tower room too?" she asked.

"Of course. The castle penthouse."

She laughed and gripped his hand more tightly, leaned in and pressed her face against his shoulder as they walked quickly up the next flight of stairs.

He reached into his pocket and pulled out an old-fashioned key and put it into the lock. She watched his hands as he turned the key, watched his olive skin stretch over the muscle and tendon. He was so strong. So masculine. Sexier than any person had a right to be.

Internal muscles clenched as she remembered just how masculine he was everywhere. As she remembered what it was like to be filled by him.

He opened the door and she grabbed his hand, pulling him inside. He shut it quickly and wrapped his arms around her waist, twirling her and pressing her back flat against the wooden door.

His kiss was urgent, hungry. There was no restraint. Which was good, because she was fresh out of restraint herself.

She fumbled with his tie, jerked it to the side and loosened it, letting it hang slack while she worked at the buttons on his crisp white shirt. She nearly whimpered out loud when she revealed that toned, muscular chest.

This time she was really going to explore him, take her time and enjoy that gorgeous body. She spread her hands over his chest, felt his heart raging beneath her palms.

"You really do want me," she said, sliding her hands from his chest, down to where his erection was pressing against his black slacks. She cupped his heavy weight and he sucked in a sharp breath.

"I do," he said, teeth clenched.

"Take me."

He didn't waste any time accepting her invitation. He swept her up into his arms and carried her to the bed, depositing her gently on the edge. He worked at discarding his tie, jacket, and shirt, throwing them into a careless heap on the floor. Then he kicked off his shoes and socks.

She reached out and put her hands on his belt, undoing it quickly before she shoved his pants and underwear down to the floor.

She wrapped her hand around his hard length, stroked him, reveled in the grunt of pleasure he made in the back of his throat. The desire to taste him, to do what he'd done to her in his office, overwhelmed her.

She'd never wanted to do this for a man before. Had only ever tolerated doing it for the one man she'd been with before Aleksei. But she wanted Aleksei. Wanted so badly to pleasure him. And she wanted it for herself.

Leaning in, she flicked her tongue over the velvety head of his shaft, her hands still cupping him. He jerked, a raw sound escaping his lips. Emboldened, she continued to explore him with her lips and tongue until he gripped her wrists and pulled her away.

"Not like that. Not this time."

She shook her head. She was on the same page with him, one hundred percent. She needed him inside of her.

He sat beside her on the bed, pulling the zipper on her dress down. She stood and let it fall into a pool of black taffeta at her feet. She was gratified by the heat in his gaze, by the pure, undisguised hunger she saw etched into every line of his gorgeous, naked body.

"You didn't have anything under that dress all night?" he asked, voice rough.

She gave him her best seductive smile. "I had a mission. Underwear wasn't conducive to my end goal."

"Vixen," he grated.

She reached around to grasp the clasp of the necklace.

"Leave it," Aleksei ground out.

She dropped her hands to her sides. For a moment he only stared at her. Her nipples peaked, ached, and she was so hot and ready for him it was amazing. The fact that she didn't want to cover her body was a testament to how bold, how different he made her feel.

"Come here, Maddy," he said from his place on the edge of the bed.

She complied, toeing off her high heels and kneeling on the bed, straddling his body. He put his hands on her hips and tilted his face up so he could kiss her. Slowly, thoroughly. She gripped his shoulders to keep herself from melting at his feet.

He moved his attentions lower, pressing a hot kiss to the curve of her neck, her collarbone just above the necklace.

Then he turned his attention to her breasts. He stroked one nipple with the flat of his tongue before drawing it into his mouth. His teeth scraped the necklace, and her flesh, lightly and she shivered.

He turned his attention to her other breast, where he was just as thorough. He lifted his head for a moment. "I forgot to do this last time, and it has been the staple of my fantasies ever since."

"It was a good one," she said, her voice shaking.

He lay back on the bed and brought her with him. She was astride him, his erection pressing against the part of her that was slick with her desire for him. He scooted them both back and reached into the nightstand that was positioned by the big bed. He grabbed a condom out of the drawer and handed it to her.

She tore it open without wasting any time and rolled it onto his hard length, protecting them both from any consequences. That was the last thing either of them needed.

He put his hands on her hips and helped guide himself into her body. They both made noises of pleasure as he slid into her.

She was almost frantic in her movements at first. She was so desperate for release. Now that she knew what she was after, it was much easier to find the right rhythm. It helped that Aleksei was stroking her clitoris with his thumb as she moved.

"Like that?" he asked, his dark eyes locked with hers.

"Yes, oh, yes," she panted.

He moved his other hand up her back, caressing the dent of her waist before cupping her breast. He teased one hardened bud, moving one of the gems from the necklace over her sensitive skin. The chill from the gold contrasted with the heat of his touch, the stimulation enough to send her over the edge.

As she cried out her release, Aleksei took control, rolling them so that he was in the dominant position and she was on her back. He thrust hard into her and she wrapped her legs tightly around his waist, the aftershocks of her orgasm still pulsing through her as he established his own rhythm, brought himself to the peak of pleasure.

All she could hear was their mingled breathing and the pounding of her heart. Aleksei drew her into his arms and maneuvered them so that she was partially on top of him, their bodies no longer connected.

They stayed that way for a moment before Aleksei sat up. She sat too, intending to collect her gown and get dressed again before heading back to her room.

"No," he said firmly, standing from the bed. "I'm going to take care of things." Meaning the condom, she assumed. "And you're staying."

"You want me to share your bed?" It seemed an intimacy farther than they should take it, and yet part of her wanted to stay with him. Stay near his warmth. Maybe wake up to the kind of pleasure they'd just shared.

She'd never actually slept with a man before. The hazard of having a married lover. Something always came up. Something that meant he had to leave the hotel room. Another clear and obvious sign she'd missed.

She shook her head. She wasn't going there.

"Okay. I'll stay."

CHAPTER NINE

It was still dark when Maddy woke up. Aleksei's arm was curled around her waist and she was fitted snugly against his body. For a moment she just enjoyed the feeling. Being so close to someone else. Skin to skin. Breathing the same air.

It was amazing.

And then, suddenly, the intimacy of it felt like too much to handle.

She wiggled out of his grasp and climbed out of bed, unsure of what she was going to do. The bathroom was the logical first stop. She tiptoed into the room and closed the door behind her.

She took care of the necessities and then washed her hands before pooling cool water in her palms and splashing it on her face. She stood and faced her reflection. She looked thoroughly seduced. Her hair was a disaster, there were remnants of last night's eye makeup on her cheeks and she was still wearing a necklace worth more money than she would ever see in her life.

Reaching around, she unhooked the necklace and decided that figuring out where Aleksei was keeping valuables was next on her to-do list before she made her escape.

When she crept back into the bedroom, gray light was filtering in through the large windows. She swore under breath when she noticed her black gown in a pool of fabric on the floor.

There was nothing else for her to wear. She had come to Aleksei's room in a ball gown, and panty-less, and now she had nothing to return to her room in. There were probably still guests and paparazzi milling around.

The walk of shame indeed.

She looked back at the bed, at the man sleeping there, the covers pushed low on his hips, his upper body bare. What she really wanted to do was crawl back into bed and wake him up in a very creative way.

Instead, she decided to clean up the mess they'd made the night before. She placed the necklace on the nightstand. Aleksei could put it in a safe when he woke up.

She sighed and bent down, picking up her ball gown and shaking out the wrinkles as best as she could before laying it over the back of a chair. She kicked her shoes under the writing desk, then picked up Aleksei's pants, placing them over her dress.

When she went to pick up Aleksei's suit jacket, she noticed a short length of chain lying next to it. She picked it up and moved her hands over it. It wasn't just chain, but in the dim light it was hard to tell what it was.

She turned on the lamp that was on the writing desk and held her find beneath the light. It wasn't a simple chain at all. It was art. Twisting vines, complete with thorns and subtle small flowers sculpted into the leaves, the centers made from varying shades of pink gemstones, the petals fashioned from seed pearls and diamonds. There were hundreds of blossoms, each so delicate and tiny that the little piece of necklace wasn't gaudy at all. It was a study in subtle beauty. It was only on closer inspection that the labor, the design, was evident.

Aleksei had made it. Had started it. It was obvious. The jewelry he designed was more beautiful than any she'd seen, but this surpassed even what she'd seen of his work. There was something more in it.

"What are you doing with that?" Aleksei's voice, clipped and harsh, startled her and she whirled around to face the bed.

He was sitting, his dark eyes locked onto the small piece of jewelry in her hands.

"It was on the floor," she said.

He looked at her for a long moment and then held out his hand. She crossed to the bed and dropped the length of chain into his upturned palm. He didn't say anything and neither did she. He ran his thumb over the chain, his expression still, eyes distant, mouth tight.

"It is designed to look like *salsola*," he said, his voice rough. "A common weed in Russia. Common in many parts of the world."

"It's too beautiful to be a weed," she said.

A soft laugh escaped his lips. "Yes, some people think that." He let out a heavy breath. "My wife thought so. They grew outside of our home in Russia. She would never let me destroy them."

Her stomach twisted. Wife? He didn't have a wife. He couldn't have a wife. No one, not even she, was that stupid to make the same mistake twice.

"You…you're not married," she said, her voice barely a shaking whisper.

"No, I'm not," his tone was heavy. Final.

Silence settled between them. The question of what

had happened hovered on her lips, and yet she couldn't make herself ask. Because she knew, by the way he'd said he wasn't married, that the union had not been dissolved by the court system.

"How long?" They were the only words she could force around the lump in her throat.

"Six years." He set the necklace segment on the nightstand. "I was making this for her. It was meant to be a surprise."

But she'd never got it. And he had never finished it.

It had been in his jacket pocket. Close to his heart.

Maddy put a hand to her chest, to where her own heart felt battered, bruised and bleeding. Not for herself, for Aleksei. Just as she'd felt his humor resonating in her the night before, she felt his grief now. Real. Raw. Deep.

"I...I didn't know."

"It's not a secret. I don't make conversation about it, but it was in the news when it happened. Though, at the time, my success was limited, and my name was only really known in Russia, which means it likely wasn't international news. Although, I honestly couldn't tell you. Media coverage wasn't on my mind at the time."

Six years. It had been six years since he'd designed a collection, until recently. It suddenly made horrible, painful sense. He hadn't designed, but he'd grown his company. Had found worldwide success.

But he'd lost his wife.

"Paulina was killed in a car accident," he said. "I knew you wouldn't ask. It's why this can never be more than this." He gestured to the bed. "I've done commitment. I've done marriage. I won't do it again. I can't."

Her throat was tight, aching. For him. "I don't...I

don't want you to. I don't want to marry you. I don't even believe in love."

"I do. But that part of my life is over."

She gritted her teeth, fought against the pressing weight of pain she felt for him, and against the sense of debt that she felt now. This was why she hadn't wanted to know the reason he didn't do relationships. Because of the emotions churning inside of her.

Because then she would have to tell him why *she* didn't do relationships. Would have to lay bare the most humiliating moment of her life. Would have to reveal her stupidity, her weakness. Would have to admit why she'd been vulnerable to a man like William in the first place.

Her stomach lurched.

"Madeline, come here."

She moved to the bed, her heart hammering so hard she was sure he could hear it. She climbed up and got under the covers. He pulled her to him and kissed her.

"The past doesn't matter. It's over," he said. "What we have is right now. We both understand what this is. We both want the same thing."

She kissed him desperately, passionately. She could handle this. Sex. Need. Lust.

She shoved all of the pain to the side, all of the things she was feeling, for him, for herself, and just embraced her need.

It was all she could handle.

That Madeline had withdrawn after she'd found out about Paulina shouldn't bother Aleksei at all. And yet he found that it did. He didn't talk about his wife. He certainly didn't show anyone the piece of the necklace he'd been designing for her.

He didn't carry it out of grief. Paulina had been gone six years, and while he still regretted her death, the acute pain had faded a few years ago. He carried it as a reminder of what happened when you let yourself love someone.

When someone became your whole world and that world crumbled around you.

Paulina's death had nearly destroyed him at the time. He'd spent a year drinking too much and trying to forget, wallowing in his misery.

And then he'd realized he was going to die along with her if he didn't move forward. Since that moment, he'd moved forward. He'd picked up where he'd left off with his fledgling design company, had finally found the worldwide recognition he'd been trying to achieve before Paulina's death.

He'd succeeded in business. He'd made millions. And while none of it was what he'd dreamed it would be when he was a young man, it was better than falling into the abyss.

Success had been his antidote to depression. He'd simply never stopped, even when it wasn't necessary to his survival to keep climbing the ladder.

He saw elements of that in Madeline. She always seemed to have her armor on. And it bothered him that it mattered at all.

There was a soft knock on his office door.

"Come in."

He looked up and saw Madeline slipping in, looking thoroughly respectable in a tight knee-length skirt and a sweater. So respectable all he could think of was making her look a bit more disreputable.

They hadn't made love since they'd left Luxembourg four days earlier and he was surprised at how much he missed her touch. He'd gone for very long periods of time without sex. Two years after losing Paulina. But for some reason, these four days had seemed like an eternity.

He didn't want to examine why that was. Why he responded to her with such intensity.

"We have a slight problem with the venue for the Paris exhibition."

"Do we?" Aleksei leaned back in his chair and tried to focus his mind on the task at hand, and not on Madeline's gorgeous body. On how much he would like to undo the top button on her prim little sweater…

"Yes. They're double booked. And they want one of us to shuffle the time."

He leaned forward and put his hands on his desk. "The other event can shuffle."

"That's what I said."

"And?"

"And they gave me a very non-committal answer. Said I would have to take it up with Oracle. That would be the company that is also booked for Le Grande ballroom on the same date we have Le Grande ballroom booked."

"I figured as much," he said wryly, pressing his palms firmly on the desk and standing. "What's the number?"

She handed him her cellphone and indicated her last outgoing call. He highlighted the number and pressed Send.

What followed was a flurry of French that Madeline

couldn't understand. She spoke a little bit of French, but it was about as good as her Italian. Which wasn't very good, and certainly not proficient enough to engage in serious business negotiations.

When Aleksei hung up he handed her the phone again, his fingers brushing hers, little rivulets of pleasure traveling up her arm and through her body. She could have purred, it felt so good.

And, for the moment, she wasn't going to try and fight the attraction between them. They hadn't had a chance to be together since the exhibition in Luxembourg, but she was still in full *embrace the fling* mode.

"Success?" she asked, putting her phone back in her pocket.

"Of course."

Of course. Spoken like a man who never expected to be told no. A man who had complete control over every aspect of his life and was completely confident in that.

Except he hadn't always had control. Her heart ached when she thought of his wife, of the pain he'd been through. It disturbed her, just how much it weighed on her.

She smiled. "Of course."

He rounded his desk and took her in his arms. He didn't kiss her, not immediately. He simply rested his head on her hair, his hands stroking her back, warm and comforting. She inhaled his scent, so familiar, so exciting.

When he did kiss her, he put his thumb and forefinger on her chin and tilted her face up, pressing his lips lightly against hers.

"I've missed you," he said.

"Me too." The words were a whisper. An admission

that was difficult for her to make, both to him and to herself.

"I need you tonight," he said roughly, kissing her again, this time with very little of the restraint he'd shown the first time.

"Yes," she said, between kisses.

"I have a suite booked at the Hotel Del Sol."

Her heart sank into her stomach. She tried, she tried really hard, to shake off the nausea that gripped her. Aleksei didn't have a wife at home he was hiding from her, and what had she expected? That he would invite her back to his Milan apartment? Like she would invite him to hers? She wouldn't. It would be bringing him into her space, and that just didn't seem like something people involved in a purely sexual relationship would do.

It didn't help. She was afraid she would be sick.

"I… Maybe not tonight," she said, her voice strangled.

She noticed a muscle tick in his jaw and he loosened his hold on her. Pulled away. "A suite doesn't suit you, Madeline? Or is the hotel simply not grand enough?"

"Stop it, Aleksei, I've never behaved that way, and you know it."

Hurt, hurt that had nothing to do with him, an old wound she still carried because of her own stupidity, fueled her anger at him.

He looked away. "If you're busy, you're busy."

"I am," she said stiffly.

"See you tomorrow, Madeline." He went back to the other side of his desk and sat, turning his attention to the computer monitor.

Dismissed. He'd dismissed her. That was loud and clear.

And she was the one who had said no, so what right did she have to be angry and hurt? She gritted her teeth and stalked out of his office.

It didn't matter if she had no right to be angry and hurt. She was.

No matter how much she didn't want to be, she was.

Aleksei didn't beg for women to come to him. They just came to him. That was his experience in life, even before he'd had money. It had only been more frequent since he'd made his first million.

But he was on the verge of begging. His body was unfulfilled and sleep eluded him. He had been cold to Madeline, and then, in the end, he had seen pain in her eyes, pain that went deeper than their simple argument.

And he had turned away. Because he hadn't signed on for her pain. And now it was eating at him from the inside out.

That and the arousal that was coursing through him.

His finger hovered over the speed dial he had programmed in his phone for her.

A picture of her, naked with her black gown pooled at her feet, flashed into his mind, mingled with the image of her standing in his office, devastation in her blue eyes.

He dialed. Pride be damned.

"Hello?" She sounded as though she'd been sleeping. Or crying. His stomach twisted at the thought. Causing Madeline pain was not something he wanted any part in.

"Maddy."

"Aleksei," she said, her voice guarded. "It's past eleven."

"I know. Will you come to my apartment? It's above the studio."

"I…yes."

"Do you need me to send a car?"

He heard rustling, probably covers, in the background. "No. I can drive. I'll be there in ten minutes."

It was a long ten minutes. When he heard the buzzer, he let her in quickly, and when she came to his apartment door he already had it open for her.

He pulled her to him, kissed her. Thoroughly. She wrapped her arms around his neck and pressed her sweet body against his.

"Come in," he said.

She complied and he closed the door behind her. He was short on patience. He'd needed her hours ago, and he needed her even more now.

"The living area isn't very nice," he said, taking her by the hand. "I'll show you my bedroom."

A smile spread across her face, her eyes crinkling in the way they did when she was truly happy. She laughed. "Smooth, Aleksei."

"But it worked, right?"

Her smile broadened. "Of course."

He led her across the vast, open living area and to the double doors that partitioned his bedroom from the rest of the apartment. He didn't usually bring women to any of his personal residences. Hotels were his first choice. And yet he didn't feel as though Madeline was invading. It didn't feel like an imposition to have her.

Of course, for all the time he spent in Milan it might as well be a hotel.

"I like this," she said, looking around his bedroom. "Very manly."

He laughed. "Is it? I paid someone to decorate it."

She smiled and took her jacket off, tossing it on the chair that was positioned near his bed. "Well, they did a good job. The bed is certainly inviting. Though that may be the company, rather than the silky black bedspread. Although, the bedspread helps."

He pulled her into his arms, forked his fingers in that glossy dark hair and kissed her. Kissed her with all of the hunger that was threatening to consume him.

She kissed him back, her hands cupping his face, her soft thumbs caressing his jawline. He lowered her onto the bed and she gave a little shriek when her back hit the mattress. He chuckled and kissed her neck.

"Oh, yes, you're very smooth," she said, wrapping her arms around his neck and drawing her thighs up, parting them so he could settle between them.

He couldn't remember the last time he'd laughed with a woman. The last time sex had felt personal. The last time it had mattered who it was with.

Yes, he could. The last time he'd been with Maddy.

And then thought was impossible to think, because she was pulling his T-shirt over his head and throwing it aside, putting her hands on his chest, exploring him. Torturing him.

"*Milaya moya*, you're lethal," he said, taking her top and tugging it over her head, revealing her hot pink bra and perfect cleavage.

He made quick work of the bra and exposed her gorgeous breasts to his gaze. No dessert had ever been more tempting.

"What does that mean?" she asked, voice breathy as he feathered kisses over the tops of her breasts.

"It means *my sweet*," he said, running his tongue over one of her perky pink nipples. "And you are very, very sweet."

He tugged her jeans off, taking her panties with them and leaving her completely naked. Then he turned his attention back to her breasts. She arched beneath him and her sweet sounds of pleasure gratified him in ways he hadn't imagined were possible. It was always important to him to make sure his partner enjoyed being with him, but it had never felt as essential to his own enjoyment as it did now.

He ran his hands over her body, drew away slightly so he could admire her. Pale skin, full breasts and a flat stomach. She was so beautiful. So perfect.

Desire roared through him. He kissed her stomach, her skin so soft and tender. She wiggled beneath him, forked her fingers through his hair as he began moving his exploration to lower territory.

He loved the taste of her, loved the sounds she made when he caressed her clitoris with the flat of his tongue.

She tugged on his shoulders slightly. "Now," she said. "Please. I need you now."

He stood and took his wallet out of his pocket and set in on the bed before shucking his jeans and underwear and consigning them to the floor with the rest of the clothes.

He opened his wallet and pulled out a condom.

"I've got it," she said, getting up on her knees and taking the packet from his hand.

She opened it and rolled it onto his length. She wasn't overly experienced. He'd realized that the last time they were together. But her confidence along with her obvious desire more than made up for it. And the fact that she tackled the condom application slowly only made it an even sweeter torture.

He lowered himself over her, kissed her and she lay back, parting her thighs for him. He tested her, felt how ready she was before thrusting into her in one motion.

"Oh, yes," she sighed, gripping his shoulders, her nails digging into his skin. The slight pain was just enough to help offset the blinding pleasure, enough to keep him from ending things much too quickly.

She locked her legs around his calves, her head thrown back in obvious pleasure. He kissed her neck, her collarbone, her lips, as he established a rhythm that drove them both to the edge.

She arched beneath him, panting in his ear, her sounds of pleasure the thing that pushed him over, forced him to give up and embrace the hot rush of his orgasm. She followed, her internal muscles clenching tight around him, the pleasure more intense than anything he'd experienced before.

He rolled to the side and pulled her to him. She cuddled against him, her breath hot against his chest.

"I'm sorry about before," she said quietly, her words muffled.

"I hurt you, Maddy. I'm not proud of that, even if I don't know the reason why you were hurt."

She sucked in a sharp breath. "It…it wasn't really your fault. There's no reason you should know why."

He clenched his teeth. Part of him wanted to press for more. The other part wanted to kiss her again, to make it up to her in the best way he could think of. He didn't do pillow talk. Didn't mine his lovers for information.

"Who hurt you?" He tightened his grip on her. And he realized he wanted to know. He wanted to know so he could kill whoever it was that had put that look in Maddy's eyes. And he wanted to be sure he wasn't the man who had put it there.

She laughed shakily and rolled away from him. "That's a loaded question."

He was caught between the desire to tell her that her secrets were hers to keep, and the need to know more. The need to try and slay her dragons.

He turned so that he was on his side, facing her. "That's okay."

"I guess we can start with my parents," she said, not looking at him. "They just didn't… They weren't really all that into kids, and I was a late-in-life surprise. They had already raised my brother, and they didn't really want… I'm fifteen years younger than Gage. They were done by then."

Aleksei's heart squeezed tight. He shouldn't have asked. What could he do to soothe her pain? Nothing. He had nothing to give. And in Maddy, in this moment, he sensed so much need. So much need he would be unable to meet.

"Anyway, when I was ten they went on a trip…I don't even know what it was for. But they'd let my nanny go and the new one hadn't arrived. I was alone for three days with no food. Not because there was no money. There was lots of money. They just…forgot. I called Gage and he came and got me. I never went back to that house."

There was no pain in her voice, no emotion at all.

It was something he knew well. That complete separation from all feelings. Because the other option was to be consumed by misery. And it was obvious neither of them had allowed that. They had moved on. They had chased success and found it rather than embracing destruction.

"Gage made things nice for me," she continued, her voice steady. "He even made sure I went to prom. I don't know if he paid my date to take me, or if it was a dare, but at least I went. I was… I had a hard time with friends and boys because I just didn't…think very much of myself, for obvious reasons. I mean, if your parents don't want you it's hard to believe anyone will. And then I met William."

Adrenaline spiked through Aleksei's system. He knew, just by the way she said the other man's name, that he was going to be fighting the urge to commit a murder by the end of the story.

"He was my boss when I graduated from college. I got an internship. He was really nice to me, always complimenting me and telling me I was beautiful. When he started making advances I was really flattered…and it was so nice to have someone just…want me. No one else had ever…wanted me."

She turned away from him. "I was so stupid, Aleksei. I just wanted to be loved. I was so desperate for it. My parents wouldn't give it to me, and this man was…he was older and powerful and handsome and he said he loved me."

"A lot of young girls make that mistake," Aleksei said, voice rough.

Madeline sat up, letting the covers fall to her waist. "Yes, a lot of girls throw their virginity away on men who profess love but are just using them, I know that. But not a lot of girls break up marriages. I did. And it was in the papers, headline news, because his wife was this semi-famous model and actress. And for a few months I got to be infamous."

"He was married?" Dark rage roiled in his gut. He marveled at the fact that only moments ago he'd considered himself a man with complete dominion over his emotions. That control was gone. If he ever met that man in person…he could not be responsible for what he would do to him.

"I didn't know he was married. I don't think I did anyway. Sometimes I wonder now if I just let myself be ignorant. I didn't talk to the other employees. I didn't tell anyone about William and me. I didn't question him when he took me to hotels and then left right…after. That's my deep dark secret. Although, if you'd looked me up on Google, you might have found it. Even though it's been five years."

Aleksei looked at her, at her still, tense body. She was still waiting for censure, for him to side with the press.

"It doesn't matter what you knew or didn't know, Maddy." Aleksei sat up and moved toward her. "A man is responsible for keeping his own marriage vows. I never strayed when I was married. I loved my wife, and no one could have enticed me to betray the promises I made to her."

"But I…" Her expression was bleak. "I just should have…I should have made a better choice."

"He took advantage of you. I cannot respect a man who preys on anyone's weaknesses, especially not those of a vulnerable girl. He is not worthy to call himself a man."

She looked down, dark lashes fanning over high cheekbones. "No one else saw it that way. I've never seen it that way. The headlines were right. I'm a home-wrecker."

"The press loves scandal, loves a villain. But don't let them decide how you see yourself. Your boss, he was the home-wrecker."

Maddy drew her knees up to her chest. Her heart was racing, her hands shaking. She'd never told anyone the full story of her life. Not about her parents. Not about William. But it had all come pouring out of her now. Every ugly truth. And Aleksei wasn't looking at her in disgust. His dark gaze was almost tender. She couldn't understand it. Any of it.

As much as it had hurt to see the headlines, it had felt like penance. It had felt necessary. She had embraced the guilt, because it had helped to block out the pain of her broken heart.

"Do you know the worst thing?" she asked, almost desperate for Aleksei to condemn her, to confirm her guilt. "He came to me, after the story broke about the affair. He said he loved me. He said he wanted me to stay with him." She felt a tear slide down her cheek, but she ignored it. "I was tempted. I didn't want to lose him. I didn't want to lose those feelings. He told me how beautiful I was and how special…I think I loved that more than I ever loved him."

"That's why you have so much trouble accepting compliments from me."

Again, Aleksei didn't condemn.

"Yes. They didn't mean anything from William.

They were just a means of controlling me. And it worked. The word *love* is more effective at keeping someone prisoner than chains. I was so…desperate. I hate that part of myself. I've done everything I could since then to just not need."

Aleksei just looked at her, his dark eyes unreadable.

"How can you not hate me for everything I've just told you?" she asked.

"Because you don't deserve that, Maddy." He extended his arms, pulled her to him. She crumpled against him, letting a few more tears slip down her cheeks. "You didn't deserve any of it. Not the way your parents treated you, not the way he manipulated you. And you need to see yourself as you are. You *are* beautiful."

Her lungs felt like they might burst and her heart ached. The emotions in her felt too big to be contained. Grief. Anger. Acceptance.

And something else, something that frightened her with its strength.

More tears escaped and, for a while, she simply let them come. She needed the release, needed to wash away the guilt that had lived in her for so long.

She had been a victim then. Young and naive. Both as a neglected child, and then as an emotionally needy adult. But she couldn't let those things control her anymore. She had to let it go. Really let it go.

After the storm inside of her passed, Aleksei still held her, his body warm and comforting against hers.

She inhaled his scent. Deep comfort spread through her, different than she'd ever experienced before. Peace that went deeper than she'd ever known. He simply held her in the silence, and nothing had ever meant more to her.

"You know," she said softly. "You gave me my first orgasm."

A one-note chuckle escaped his lips. "What?"

"I just thought you should know that."

"Now I really want to kill the bastard."

"Why is that?" she asked.

"The least he could have done was made some effort for you."

"At this point, it doesn't matter. I'm happy to have learned all I have from you."

She snuggled into him. At the moment, she was simply happy to be with him. In the morning, maybe she would examine that. And maybe she would even panic. But for now, she was simply going to enjoy.

CHAPTER TEN

"LET's go out today," Aleksei said from his position on the couch.

Maddy turned to face Aleksei, shocked that he hadn't sent her packing yet. She'd spent the night in his apartment, an apartment he'd been reluctant to invite her to. And then he'd fixed her breakfast, brought it to her in bed.

Now it was nearing noon and he still didn't seem to be champing at the bit to be rid of her. And now he was suggesting they spend the actual day together. Out of bed. Seemed like a violation of 'strictly sexual fling' rules to her. There were rules, she was sure of it. A more experienced woman would know.

"You want to go out?" She walked around the kitchen counter and joined him on the couch in the living room. "We could stay in."

He kissed her lightly on the lips. "Yes, we could. But I want to take you out."

She sucked in a breath. It was noticeably easier to do today than it had been yesterday. As though a weight had been removed from her. In a way, that was exactly what had happened. She'd finally been able to let go of the things that had been holding her back for so many years.

It was only natural she feel lighter. Freer than she'd ever felt before.

"I only have a T-shirt and jeans. Unless you want to stop by my house." She'd rushed over last night, not even bothering with makeup or perfume or any of the things a man of Aleksei's caliber might expect from a mistress.

But he'd wanted her anyway. He'd said she was beautiful. He hadn't judged her.

Her chest felt tight, as though it were too full. It was the strangest feeling. Foreign. Completely new to her. And she had a feeling she didn't want to know the name for it.

Instead of dwelling on it, she took another sharp breath and tried to ease the feeling of fullness.

"I think you're quite sexy in your jeans," he said.

She laughed. She couldn't help it. She just felt happy. She had felt happy since the moment she'd decided to start up her strictly sexual relationship with Aleksei. It was probably part of that feeling of lightness.

"Then as long as you're up for casual we're good to go."

Aleksei took her hand in his and squeezed it, looking right at her, his dark eyes intense, as he lowered his head and pressed a kiss to her palm. "It pleases me to do whatever suits you today."

She pulled her hand away and kissed him on the mouth, trying to ignore the hammering of her heart. Trying to ignore the way she felt when he looked at her like that. When he said things that clearly went beyond the borders of the bedroom.

* * *

The antiques market at the Naviglio canal was packed, people walking shoulder to shoulder, the noise of voices, shouting, laughing, talking, making it hard to hear Maddy speak right next to him.

He had never enjoyed things like this. He'd always preferred intimate restaurants, private dining if possible, or small gatherings of people. But the look on Maddy's face made it worth it. Her blue eyes were sparkling as they wandered around looking at different stalls, stopping to admire treasures at all of the booths.

Unless they were in bed, it was rare for him to see her so relaxed. Her dark hair was loose and messy from the breeze and she had pink residue on her lips from the candy floss she'd been eating. And she was smiling.

He was glad to give her a reason to smile. No one else in her life had. He felt the hot burn of anger rising in him again when he thought of all of the people who had wronged Madeline. Fate was cruel. No question.

What had happened to Paulina was proof enough of that. His wife had been so young, with so much yet ahead of her. And it had all been taken away in an instant.

And then there was Maddy. Thank God for her brother or she would have had no one. Would she even have survived her childhood? He knew of her family. They were wealthy, society's elite. And they had left their daughter alone with no food.

He tightened his hands into fists. Then there was her former boss. The man who had taken such perfect, sick advantage of a young girl who had been so neglected that she had been starving for affection. And he had known it.

The bastard.

That was why he was here, at the market. Because she deserved something that made her smile. She deserved to be happy. For someone to treat her with consideration. He couldn't love her, couldn't give her everything she deserved. But he could give her this.

He could make her happy for a few moments in time.

He noticed her blue eyes light up when she saw the large tourist-filled boats moored in the canal. The men in the boats were charging an exorbitant sum for a ten-minute ride, but money was not one of his concerns.

"Would you like a ride?"

She looked at him, her expression so open and sweet it made his stomach clench tight. "It's such a tourist thing."

He shrugged. "Technically, I'm a tourist. I don't spend all that much time in Milan, and you've only been living here for what? Three months? We're both tourists."

She put her hand on her chin as though she was considering it. "True. Okay."

"That didn't take much convincing," he said as he paid one of the men and helped Maddy down into the boat.

She cuddled up against him, looping her arms through his. "I know, but I really wanted to go."

He chuckled, surprised by how easy it was. "I could tell."

It was a silly thing to do, Maddy acknowledged as the boat slid smoothly through the smooth water of the canal. But it was also romantic. A silly smile spread over her face and she pressed her face against Aleksei's shoulder. It didn't even matter that there were ten other people in the boat. She could barely see them. Not when Aleksei was so close.

Dimly, it registered that she shouldn't be looking for romance. She should be running from it. That wasn't part of the bargain at all. Because romance was coupled with love more often than not, and she just…she still didn't trust herself enough.

She'd forgiven herself for what had happened with William, but she should still learn from it. Her desire to be loved had overridden common sense. It had made her behave stupidly, and she had no desire to go there again.

But that wasn't what this was about. This was about the moment. About being with Aleksei. Their relationship was temporary. It would end when one of them tired of the other one. She knew that now, so there would be no heartbreak later.

She felt a slight ache in her chest and she ignored it. She wasn't going to be heartbroken. Of course, it was hard to imagine tiring of Aleksei. He was just so good in bed. And he was sweet. Considerate. No one had ever taken her to anything like this before. No one had ever indulged her with a boat ride through Milan. Her parents…they never would have taken her to something like this in the first place.

Gage had been so good to her, but he had been so young, he just hadn't thought to provide anything extra. Just having her had been all he could handle, and she had been far too timid to ask. Why would she when, in her mind, no one had time for her?

And with William, everything had been clandestine. So there certainly hadn't been any dates.

So it was natural that she would miss this, would

miss him, a little when it came to an end. She suppressed a sigh.

The boat came to a stop where they had started, the short loop completed. Aleksei stood and got out, stepping up on to the stone walkway before reaching down to help her. She gripped his hand and let him pull her up, but her shoe slipped on the edge of the slick stone, she banged her knee on the rock edge of the canal and scraped her other leg down the side of the rough stone before crashing back into the boat, onto the green vinyl covered benches, barely missing another passenger.

"Ow," she said, trying to stand again.

Aleksei was back in the boat in a second, barking angry Italian at the concerned tour guide. He knelt down beside her, his dark eyes fierce. "Are you okay, Maddy?"

"I'm…ouch…I'm fine. I mean, it hurts, but I'm not mortally wounded."

He bent and scooped her into his arms. She squeaked and grabbed onto his shirt as he moved into a standing position and stepped up and back onto solid ground.

"I'm fine," she repeated, when a minute had gone by and he still hadn't put her down.

He narrowed his dark eyes and set her down.

"Ouch!" she said when she put weight on the knee she'd hit hardest.

"You're not fine," he said, his voice harsh.

"Nothing's broken!" she protested.

"You don't know that."

She let out an exasperated breath. "Um, yes, I'm pretty sure I do know that since I'm not incapacitated by pain."

"But it hurts when you put weight on it," he said,

wrapping an arm around her waist and helping her walk through the tight knot of people.

"Yes, probably because I have a serious bruise. But nothing more fatal than that."

"Come over here." He led her through the crowd and into a less populated part of the square. "Sit," he said, gesturing to one of the benches.

"Yes, master," she said, but she complied, because her knee really did hurt. And her other leg stung horribly, and she knew she really needed a bandage. Or three.

"Maddy," he growled.

"Sorry, but you're so intense. I fell and scraped my leg."

He knelt in front of her and rolled her jeans up slowly, careful not to scrape the rough material against her injured skin. She'd been right about the bruise. It was already turning a very unflattering color, and it was even getting swollen.

She touched the affected spot lightly. "Ow," she said.

"Well, don't touch it, Maddy," he gritted.

It was strange to see Aleksei concerned for her. He reacted to concern with anger. She realized that now. It was how he'd acted when he'd come in and seen her on the ladder. He'd been angry because he'd been... scared. For her. That was a shocking revelation.

"How is your other leg?" he asked.

She winced. "Likely bleeding."

"Let's go back to my apartment."

The walk back to Aleksei's was short, but it seemed longer thanks to the goose egg on her knee. When they were upstairs and inside, Aleksei sat her on the couch and went searching for the first aid kit. When he returned with it, he regarded her closely.

"You might need to take those off." He gestured to her jeans.

She laughed as she stood and undid the closure on her pants, trying to step out of them as carefully as possible. "Quite the bedside manner you have there."

She kicked her jeans to the side and sat back down on the couch. Aleksei crouched in front of her, propping her leg on one of his thighs as he felt around the swollen part of her knee gingerly.

"Do you feel like you need a brace?" he asked.

She shook her head. "I think I'm fine."

He moved her leg slowly and then took her other one and propped it up. She had a mean scrape down her shin that, while not as painful as the bruise, looked uglier.

He took antiseptic out of the kit and sprayed some onto her wounds. She squirmed when the cold, stinging medicine hit her skin. He looked up at her, concern in his eyes. Her heart felt so full she was afraid it was going to burst.

As Aleksei put a large piece of gauze over her scrape she felt something shift inside of her. When was the last time someone, other than her brother, had cared for her at all? There was nothing in this for Aleksei. Bandaging injuries was hardly seduction material, after all.

She swallowed hard, trying to push the lump in her throat down, trying to ignore the sting of tears she could feel welling up in her eyes. What was wrong with her? She didn't want an emotional attachment, least of all with Aleksei.

He loved his wife. He still carried the necklace.

She didn't even believe in love. She didn't. When

had she ever really seen it? Gage had been good to her, but she'd always been afraid that he…that he cared for her out of duty because he was simply too good a man to do anything less.

She took a deep breath, trying to hold back the tears. "I really… Thank you," she said, standing on wobbly legs and picking her jeans up from the floor. She tugged them on slowly, trying not to disturb her new bandages. "I should go."

"Why, Maddy? Neither of us have work tomorrow."

"Because…this is your house and I really shouldn't… impose on you anymore. You've already done more than you bargained for."

"Do you think I resent taking care of you? You're hurt."

"I…I know." That scary feeling was back, taking over, filling her.

He reached a hand out and touched her face. "Who took care of you, Maddy?"

She looked down. "My brother did. He was really good to me."

"Let me take care of you. For now, let me take care of you."

She was powerless to resist his words, powerless to deny the rising tide inside of her. She leaned in and kissed him. Kissing was good. Uncomplicated. It was a lot easier to deal with than him treating her so kindly. Taking her on a boat ride and buying her cotton candy.

It was a lot easier to deal with than the riot of emotions that were pounding through her, making her dizzy with their force.

She couldn't ignore them forever. But she would ignore them for now.

* * *

When Maddy woke up, she was naked, in Aleksei's bed, and the sun streaming through the window was fiery orange. She checked the bedside clock. It was seven in the evening. She'd slept for most of the afternoon, after they'd made love.

He'd been so gentle with her, careful because of her very minor injuries. He'd been so concerned about hurting her. She sucked in a breath, trying to ease the tension in her chest.

The bedroom door opened and Aleksei strode in from the *en suite* bathroom, a towel wrapped low around his lean hips. For a moment, all she could do was admire him. How had she got so lucky to have him for a lover? He was so beautiful.

Broad, bronzed chest bare, his muscles shifting as he walked to the bed. He was more than looks, though. He was a good boss, a savvy businessman. He was the kind of man who would get on his knees to clean your wounds.

Her breath caught.

"Feeling better?" he asked, sitting on the edge of the bed.

She pulled the covers tightly around her. "I never felt bad. You were worrying about nothing."

"I don't want to see you get hurt, Maddy."

That sounded more like a warning than anything else. And not a warning against further knee-scrapes.

"Aleksei, I know what this is. I'm the one who instigated it. I don't even believe in love."

"Not at all?"

"No. People make you love them, then they use it against you. Neglect you and remind you that they're your parents, so you love them even if they forgot to pick you up from school again. Or forgot even to send one of the household staff to get you."

"Your parents are unfit to be called human beings."

"No argument," she said.

"I believe in love," he said hoarsely.

Her stomach lurched and her heart pounded, everything in her body on hold as she waited for his next words. There was no reason for that. No reason she should be holding her breath to hear what he would say next. But she was.

"I loved my wife," he said finally. "From the moment I met her. I was eighteen. She was just sixteen. She became my world. For nine years, she was my world. I loved her so much that losing her nearly destroyed me. I know that love is real, because I've tasted the loss of it. I know what it's like for breathing to be physical pain, for it to be harder to live than to give up. That's the power of love, Maddy."

Her stomach hurt. It hurt so much to hear him say that, to know how badly he'd suffered.

"The power of love sounds dangerous," she choked.

"I'm never going through that again," he said, his voice hard, his dark eyes flat.

"Well, maybe love is real," she said softly. "But it seems like it always hurts."

"I don't hurt anymore, Maddy. I don't let myself feel enough to hurt."

Maddy nodded slowly. "I understand that. I've lived most of my life that way. The one time I tried…it didn't end well."

"I won't ever love you. But I won't lie to you either."

The stab of pain in her chest was so sharp, so real, that it shocked her. She ignored it. "That's all I've ever asked of you, Aleksei. All I've ever wanted was your honesty."

And she had it. Even now, even with her naked and in his bed, he wouldn't even profess the possibility of loving her. It was what she wanted. What she needed.

It was.

"You have that. I promise."

She thought about the necklace Aleksei carried with him. The necklace that he'd never finished. "Your wife must have been a really wonderful woman."

"Paulina knew me before I had anything. She supported me while I worked toward my crazy dreams. When she died…I was getting there, but she never saw me truly succeed. We were poor for most of our time together. We didn't have very much. We had a small house."

"With weeds in the backyard," Maddy whispered.

"Yes," Aleksei said, his voice thick.

She had the feeling that if he could trade his empire for that small house again, he would.

He was right. Love was real. And he'd had it. What could she offer him in the face of that kind of love? She was the girl not even her parents could love.

It didn't matter anyway. He was right. Love was real. And it was pain. A pain she wouldn't put herself through.

"I really should go back home," she said, swinging her legs over the side of the bed, careful of her bruise.

"Do you need a ride?" It hurt that he didn't ask her to stay.

"No. I have my car."

"I'll see you on Monday."

"You'll still be here?" she asked. That was all she

said, but it wasn't the only question she had. Were they done? Was this it?

"Until my work here is finished I won't be going back to Russia."

She hated that they were speaking in code. Even though she'd never promised him the same honesty he'd promised her, she had given it. But now she felt she was keeping something from him. She had a feeling it was the same thing she was trying to hide from herself.

"I…" Her words caught. She bent down and scooped her clothes off the floor, conscious that he was watching her and she was naked. She didn't usually feel naked in front of him. But she did now.

She dressed quickly, not about to duck into the bathroom, even though part of her wanted to. But it was silly. Obviously Aleksei didn't feel the shift that had taken place in her. He was still lounging on the bed in his towel. She wasn't about to show him how confused she was. How suddenly everything felt different to her.

"I'll see you Monday," she said softly.

He didn't say anything.

CHAPTER ELEVEN

MADDY wasn't sure what to expect from Aleksei when she came into work on Monday morning. Would he be the cold, brooding stranger he'd been when she'd left his house a couple of days earlier? Or would he be the man who'd bandaged her scraped leg? Would he be the suave lover who had seduced her in his office?

Maybe each of those men were a part of him. Well, they had to be, she supposed. There were moments, small moments, like when she'd told him about her past, when he seemed to care. Then there were moments where he seemed completely cut off from all emotion.

Just like she was. Had been? Forget who Aleksei would be today. Who was she?

She pushed the door to his office open and held out a coffee cup. "I come in peace," she said, setting it on his desk.

"I don't drink coffee," he said.

She pulled a face. "Sorry." She knew that too. He'd told her.

"Thank you," he said.

"For bringing you a drink you don't even like?"

"For the thought," he bit out. "How is everything going with the preparation for the Paris exhibition?"

"Going well now that we have the scheduling thing handled, thank you by the way, and I have the layout planned and all the decorations purchased."

"And how are you?"

"I'm fine. I don't think my leg needs to be amputated or anything." She looked at the lid of her coffee cup.

"I meant how are you? I was…I did not behave well on Saturday night."

"It's okay. We got…very heavy. It's good, I think we know we're on the same page, but maybe we need to keep things in lighter territory."

The corners of his mouth lifted, but there was no smile in his eyes. "Maybe."

"I'm… Do you want to come over tonight? I don't cook, but I have take-out restaurants on my speed dial, and I have a very experienced dialing finger."

She didn't have people over very often. Ever. But she didn't feel strange asking Aleksei to come over. It felt right. It had felt right being at his house, even though she'd been afraid to go at first. Afraid of the intimacy it might add to the relationship.

"I'll meet you there after work," he said.

"Okay."

She still felt a strange distance between them. Like something was missing. And she had no idea what it might be.

"Can you show me your plans design-wise for Paris?"

Maddy blinked and tried to bring herself back to reality, tried to get some focus on the task at hand.

"Sure, I have everything with me." She took her tablet computer out of her bag and flipped open the case. She moved through the screens quickly and brought up the sketches she'd done of the event. "I wanted to go with sort of a retro feel, but still lavish. It's like a very upscale soda shop in all black, white and pink. I think the colored gems will really stand out, and it's a completely different event to what we put on in Luxembourg. Clean lines, very chic, rather than... fairytale chic."

Although she'd been kind of fond of the fairytale.

"And what do you have here?" he asked, pointing to a shaded area of her sketch.

"Oh, this is the stage. I've booked a swing band."

"A swing band, huh?"

"Yes, it's going to be really fun. That's kind of the theme. Fun."

He laughed softly. "What do you and I know about fun, Maddy?"

"I thought we'd done a pretty good job of having it over the past week or so," she said softly, closing the case on her tablet and putting it back in her bag.

"I suppose we have." He looked at her, but his expression was distant, like he wasn't really seeing her.

She sat down in the chair in front of Aleksei's desk as he talked guest numbers, security and all the other incidentals that didn't fall under food, music and decor. She watched Aleksei's mouth as he talked. He really had a wonderful mouth.

She cleared her throat and turned her attention back to her notes. She had to keep the sex thing separate from the work thing. She really did.

"You look tired," Aleksei said.

Maddy looked up and saw him staring at her, a crease between his dark brows.

"Thanks," she said tartly.

"Are you getting enough sleep?"

She thought back to Friday night, the night she'd spent in his bed, and then to the two sleepless nights that had followed. The nights where she'd missed his body. Missed his warmth and his touch.

"I'm willing to bet that I'm not."

He stood from the desk and came to stand behind her, the weight of his hands coming to rest on her shoulders. He swept her ponytail over her shoulder then started kneading her muscles slowly, methodically, sensually.

"You're tense too," he said.

"Yeah." She sucked in a breath. "Really, though, if I gave you a massage are you telling me your muscles would be relaxed?"

"Not at all," he said, his thumbs working the knots that had been tightening in her muscles over the past couple of weeks. "Maybe you should take some vacation time after this event."

Her heart felt like it was going to burst inside of her. The way he spoke to her, so tenderly, so caring. That he noticed she was tired. That her muscles were tight. Of course, he didn't know he was responsible.

No, that wasn't fair. It wasn't Aleksei's fault that their fling was becoming a source of anxiety to her. That she missed him all night when they weren't together. That her emotions were a swirl of confusion.

He'd offered sex, he'd offered honesty, and she'd taken it. Had convinced him, and herself, that that was all she wanted from him.

But it wasn't. It really wasn't. She wanted more.

She could have laughed. She'd fancied herself in love with a man who had never done anything but lie and manipulate her. Had fallen for him, because the words had come so easily to him, and he hadn't hesitated to use them to get exactly what he'd wanted.

But Aleksei would never say the words. He would never feel them either. Not for her. She didn't even have a hope. She didn't even have a lie to cling to.

But that hadn't stopped her. It hadn't kept her from falling in love with him.

She felt dizzy all of a sudden, her pulse pounding hard in her head. She loved him. Had it only been the other day she'd told him she didn't believe in love? Had it only been recently that she'd thought love didn't exist?

She stood from her seat, slipping away from his hold. She looked at him, at his handsome face, so familiar and…essential now. Her heart seized.

How had this happened? How had he become everything?

And what was she going to do when she didn't have him anymore? Because their arrangement was temporary and no alteration in her feelings would change that. Aleksei had been perfectly honest with her from the start. He wasn't looking for permanent. Or commitment or anything resembling it.

She didn't even blame him for it. How long had she clung to all of her superficial hurt and heartbreak? How long had her own mistakes colored her life?

What Aleksei had experienced had been so much more. He had lost his wife. He had lost real love, not the illusion of it. She thought she'd known loss, pain, heartbreak. But it was nothing to what Aleksei had experienced.

She could only stare at him, all words totally frozen in her mind, unable to escape. She just wanted to look at him, memorize every minute detail of his appearance.

And at the same time she wanted to turn and run away. To forget about him. To forget that she loved him.

"I…have to go back to work," she said.

He gave her a long look, slight confusion visible in his expression. "I'll see you tonight," he said.

"Actually I can't do tonight, Aleksei. I have…work." She couldn't see him tonight. She couldn't. She had to process all of this. Figure out what it meant.

She needed distance. Needed it more than she needed her next breath.

She left his office and walked through the maze of hallways back into her office. She shut the door behind her and locked it before going to her desk and collapsing into her chair, face in her hands.

It was only then that she realized what it was she was doing.

She was running. She was always running. She'd run from her parents, understandable, since she'd been a child. But it was a demon she'd never faced. She'd run from the headlines when the affair had become public.

She was running from her feelings now.

How much longer could she run until she'd left everyone and everything behind her that meant anything? Until she collapsed with exhaustion?

She wasn't going to find out.

She was done running.

This time he wouldn't call her. No matter how much his body ached, he wouldn't give in this time. He didn't play games. She said she'd wanted a purely sexual relationship, and that meant he wasn't going to fall into any of this female manipulation.

He'd had mistresses attempt it before. Like Olivia. And they were no longer a part of his life.

Even as the thought passed through his mind, he rejected it. Never had he thought of Maddy as his mistress. Strange since it was essentially what she was. They had a physical relationship, one with terms laid out nearly as clear as if it had been a business transaction.

He knew that wasn't strictly true either. Somewhere between sex on his desk and her sharing all of her deepest, darkest secrets that had changed.

His cellphone rang and he picked it up from its position on the coffee table. "Yes?"

"Aleksei." Madeline's breathless voice shocked him, sent a surge of desire, and something infinitely more powerful, through his body.

"What is it? No problems with the planning of the Paris exhibition, are there?"

"No. Everything's fine. Well, the business stuff is fine. Can you buzz me up? I'm standing in front of the building."

He stood from the couch and walked over to the front door, pressing the button to grant her access.

"I thought you were busy," he said.

"Yes, well..." She trailed off and he could picture the faint flush of pink her cheeks would have, the small smile that told him she'd been caught. "I...I decided I had to see you."

There was a small knock at the door and he opened it. And there she was, dressed in sweats and looking more beautiful than any woman had a right to.

She looked down, then back up at him, her eyes bluer, the emotion in them so deep he had to look away.

"I had to see you," she said, her voice strong. "I couldn't stay away."

Her words, so stark and honest, no shame in them, made him feel as though a crack had opened up in the stone wall that was built around his emotions. He gritted his teeth against the sensation, fought against it.

"Aleks." She took a step toward him, touched his face with soft, tender hands. There were tears in her eyes now.

She leaned in to kiss him, her lips so sweet, her touch gentle. She slid her tongue over his lips, then into his mouth, the gentle teasing flicks heating his blood, making it pump faster. Making his heart race.

Those sweet hands slid from his face to his shoulders, over his chest and down his stomach. Her touch just enough to arouse a longing in him that didn't feel familiar at all. He couldn't recall ever feeling such a vast pit of need inside of himself. A need for her body. A need for her. A need that seemed to go beyond words.

He sucked in a sharp breath when her slender fingers brushed over his erection, still covered by layers of clothing.

She looked up at him as she stroked him, her eyes meeting his, the expression there fathomless, intense. She was making love to him. The realization hit hard. Made the dam burst. A tide of sensation flooded through him and he was powerless to do anything to stop it.

"No," he growled, not realizing he'd said it out loud until after he'd spoken.

"What?" she asked.

"Too slow," he said, taking her hands in his, capturing her slender wrists in one of his hands and holding them still while he claimed her mouth.

His kiss wasn't tender. It wasn't exploratory. It was fire, intensity. He poured out every ounce of frustration, every ounce of need that would have to go unmet, into that one kiss.

When he pulled away Maddy's eyes were round, her pink lips swollen, the color in her cheeks dark and prominent. He touched where her lips were puffy from the kiss, running his thumb gently over her reddened skin before leaning in to kiss her again.

She didn't protest. She returned his kiss. The energy coming from her was electric, vibrating through him. Challenging him.

"Bed," he grated against her lips.

"Mmm."

He scooped her up and carried her the short distance into his bedroom before setting her feet gingerly back onto the floor. She pulled her top over her head, dispensing with her bra with equal speed. He worked on his own clothes while she finished undressing.

And then she was back in his arms, soft and gloriously naked.

He cupped her tight butt with one hand, a feeling of possession rolling through him, making his pulse throb, making him ache with a need so fierce it surpassed the sexual.

No. It didn't. This was only sex. Good sex. But only sex.

He wrapped his arm around her waist and gently lowered her onto the bed. He needed to prove it. He needed to wipe every shred of feeling away. Needed the hot rush of satisfaction to remind him that this was only physical.

He drew one of her taut nipples into his mouth and exulted in the purely sexual sound that escaped Maddy's lips. She arched beneath him as he moved his fingers lightly down her belly and in between her thighs, discovering just how wet and ready she was for him.

He stroked her, calling another sound of need from her body, drawn tight as a bowstring beneath his hand. He moved his thumb over the sensitive bundle of nerves and slipped a finger deep inside of her.

Her hands went to his back, fingernails digging into his flesh.

He looked at her face, her skin flushed pink, her eyes closed, her lips parted. Seeing her so caught up in her pleasure, the pleasure he was giving her, felt like a physical kick to the stomach. Never had he seen a more beautiful sight than Maddy in the midst of such abandon.

He'd had her in his bed a few times now, but never had he seen her like this. So lost in the experience, all of her barriers down.

His stomach tightened and he had to labor to draw his next breath.

She opened her eyes, the expression in them so trusting, so full of caring. He could feel it. Could feel her emotions radiating from her. Radiating in him. His throat felt tight and his body was screaming for release, while his heart was threatening to pound out of his chest.

He moved up to capture her lips, to settle between her thighs, testing her moist entrance with the head of his erection. Heat rushed through him, physical desire strong enough to blot out everything else.

Yes. This was what he needed. It was just sex. Nothing more.

He slid into her body and she let out a little moan of ecstasy that he captured with his lips. He kissed her, sifting her silky hair through his fingers as he thrust into her.

She moved her hands over his back, fingers skimming his buttocks. Her legs locked around his calves as she moved beneath him, perky nipples rubbing against his chest.

She was perfect. Amazing. He couldn't stop himself from telling her. The words fell from his lips as pleasure built inside of him, as he continued to chase down the oblivion that an orgasm would bring.

Anything. Anything to dull the emotion that seemed to be building in his chest. His blood roared in his ears as he neared the peak, drowning out everything except the pleasure that was pounding through him.

A harsh groan escaped his lips as he poured himself into her and he felt her body lock tight beneath him, felt the pulsing of her internal muscles as she gave in to her own orgasm. He was glad she'd found satisfaction, because he'd been too caught up in his own to pay her as much attention as he should have.

She wrapped her arms around his neck and pressed a soft kiss to his cheek. He looked at her, allowed himself to really see the emotion in her eyes. The remnants of the stone wall in his chest crumbled. He was raw, exposed. He was *feeling*.

The intensity of it welled up in him, all of his emotions swirling together, impossible to identify, impossible to pick out one emotion and distinguish it from the rest.

"Aleks," she whispered, stroking his neck, running her fingers through his hair. She kissed him again slowly, sweetly.

He pulled away, rolling to the side and pushing himself into a sitting position.

He turned back to face her. The way she looked at him. With so much trust. He didn't want her to look at him that way. Didn't want to see anything but lust in those beautiful blue eyes.

She sat too, wrapped her arms around her waist, resting her head on his shoulder. He set his jaw, remained motionless. She slid her hand over his chest, her touch arousing him again already.

He moved away from her and swung his legs over the side of the bed. "I need a shower."

Maddy sat still in the center of the bed. She knew that she wasn't invited to Aleksei's shower. The sharp click of the bathroom door confirmed it.

She flopped backward, resting her head on the pillow. She contemplated getting her clothes on and going back home. That was what she would have done…yesterday. She would have run from the tension between them. It was what she had done the other day.

But she wasn't going to do that today. Yesterday, she'd assumed her relationship with Aleksei would be temporary, had counted on it. Today, she was pretty sure it was still going to be temporary, but that didn't mean she wouldn't try to change that.

It scared her, the thought of putting herself out there, laying her feelings bare. The thought of trying for forever. But at the very least, no matter what happened,

Aleksei was a man who was worthy of her love. He was worth the risk. They both were.

Even though she wasn't sure if there was any way the risk would work out.

When Aleksei came back from his shower he was still stark naked, droplets of water lingering on his skin. He strode to the bed and slid in beside her. Her heart ached. She loved him. She loved him so much.

He didn't reach for her, as she longed for him to do, didn't draw her against the warmth of his body. But he was there.

Tonight, she wouldn't rock the boat with any declarations. Tonight she would just enjoy being with him. The man she loved. The man who had taught her how to love.

Aleksei woke late, which was unusual. He always got up at six after a night of barely sleeping. But last night he'd slept. With Maddy's deep, even breathing, her scent, the warm weight of her body, he had slept for the first time in six years.

No nightmares. No ghosts.

He pushed aside the realization as he made his way from the bedroom into the kitchen, where he was greeted by a sight of surreal domesticity.

Maddy was moving around the kitchen, taking bread out of the toaster and putting it on a plate next to some scrambled eggs. She was wearing his shirt, the hem riding high on her thighs when she reached up into the cupboard and took out two mugs.

When she turned to face him, that same open, honest look on her face that she'd had last night, his chest seized.

"Good morning," she said.

"You cook?"

"Well, I eat." She walked over to the stove and took a tea kettle off of one the burners—he hadn't even known he owned a tea kettle—and poured some hot water into the mugs. "I will forgive your lack of coffee as you're a caffeine-less Philistine in practice."

She picked up the plates and stood still for a moment. "You don't have a dining room set, do you?"

"No." There was no point. Not here. He wasn't in Milan often, and when he was he didn't have guests. What was the point of owning a dining table? So he could sit at it alone?

Only this morning he could have sat with Maddy. The thought wrenched the tension in his chest even tighter.

"We'll eat in here then," she said, her voice determinedly cheerful as she carried the plates into the living room and set them on the coffee table.

She sat down next to him and pushed her food around instead of eating it. She was upset with him. But he'd never promised her anything beyond what had happened last night in the bedroom and she knew that. If she'd forgotten it now, it wasn't his fault.

"Oh." She set her plate on the coffee table and stood. "I forgot I was making you tea."

"You don't have to make me tea, Maddy."

She started to walk toward the kitchen. "Aleks, it's fine."

And there she was, calling him by a pet name, walking around in his kitchen. Making tea like she was his...

"You're not my wife, Madeline," he said, his voice low and even.

She froze, her body going stiff before she turned to face him. "I know that. I made you breakfast. I'm not trying to be your wife."

"Good. Because I have no intention of ever making you my wife, of ever making any woman my wife."

She turned away again, but not before he saw the bottomless chasm of hurt behind those blue eyes. His chest felt too full, almost painful, in response to what he witnessed there. For what he had caused.

He gritted his teeth, fought to find his control again. He was a master at controlling his emotions. He had lost his dominion over himself once and he had vowed never to do it again.

There was something about Madeline…last night he hadn't even used a condom. That never happened to him. Protection was an essential part of sex as far as he was concerned. Who could enjoy themselves with the threat of pregnancy or health issues looming?

And yet he'd forgotten last night entirely. Hadn't realized until halfway through his shower. He hadn't said anything to Maddy either. He didn't want to worry her for no reason. The odds of pregnancy were low and he was in good health.

And deep down he acknowledged he didn't want to confess that she'd made him forget. He didn't even want to confess it to himself, but he was forced to.

He heard a spoon clinking against the side of the mug as Maddy stirred the tea too vigorously. She spun around suddenly, her face a study in schooled composure.

"I know I'm not your wife, Aleksei. I'm not even applying for the position because I know you just aren't ready for that. And that's okay. Heaven knows I've held on to plenty in my life. Things that weren't as bad as what you went through. But I do care about you, and if I want to show you that I don't think you should feel threatened by it."

He stood from the couch, his blood pounding fiercely through his body. "I never asked you to care for me. I never asked you to make me breakfast. This was supposed to be a physical affair."

Maddy crossed the kitchen and stepped into the living room. Now that she was closer he noticed how pale she was, what dark circles she had under her eyes. He wanted to touch her. To offer comfort. But he was the source of her pain. It would be too perverse for him to be the one to try and erase what he had caused. What he would continue to cause by not offering her more than a cold, sexual relationship.

"I know what it was supposed to be. I was the one who laid down the terms, wasn't I? But…it's funny, and I didn't expect it, but you…you've healed me, Aleksei," she said, her voice thick with emotion. "I carried so much anger, anger at myself mostly, for what had happened in my past. And I was stuck there, in my mind the little girl that no one loved, the guilty sinner who had an affair with a married man. That was who I was. Maybe not to anyone else, not anymore, but it was who I saw. You changed that."

"No. I didn't change anything, Maddy." He was just another person in her life who had used her. Another person who would hurt her if he didn't end things.

He opened his mouth to speak the words, to tell her to go. An intense burst of pain in his chest immobilized him, stopped him from saying anything.

So Maddy pressed on. "You did. You're the last man

on earth it makes sense for me to fall in love with, but I did. I do. I love you. You were the one who showed me that love was real. That it wasn't just something people use against you. Because even now you won't use it against me. I know you won't."

"Your trust is misplaced," he growled. "As is your love."

She looked down, biting her lower lip. "I know you aren't going to get on your knee and confess your undying love, Aleksei. I don't expect that. But that doesn't mean we can't still be together for now."

"I don't think you understand," he said, ignoring the trickle of anguish that was spreading from his chest through his body. "I don't need your love. I don't want it."

"Aleksei…" She moved to him.

"Stop. Maddy, you would take so little from someone? You would take a physical affair and nothing more? Because that's all you'll ever have from me. I will never give you more. I can't. I have my mistresses long term. I find it more convenient. But it doesn't ever really matter who they are so long as they're biddable and available."

He watched the light in her eyes dim, watched her entire being shrink back.

And the trickle inside of him turned into a flood. But if he didn't do it now, if he didn't make her leave now, he would only hurt her worse later. What did one emotionally crippled man have to offer a woman like Madeline? A woman who had her own hurts. A woman who had been so badly abused by those who should have cared for her.

He could give her nothing but his own shortcomings, his own pain. His own failings as a man.

"It's never mattered to me who the woman was, as long as the sex was good."

She jerked back then, as though he had slapped her. And it took everything in him to stay rooted to the spot. To not go to her. To not comfort her. Kiss her.

He had no right to do those things. Had no right to demand love from a woman like Maddy when he could offer nothing of value in return. But he wanted to. More than anything, he wanted to.

She looked up at him, blinking furiously. Maddy wouldn't dissolve, not now. He knew that. She was too strong. Or too stubborn. Maybe both.

"You're right, Aleksei. I…I am selling myself short. I deserve to be loved, not to just give it. I've given it all of my life, and the only person who ever really gave it back was my brother. Everyone else just took what I would offer and used it against me. And I always thought that meant there was something wrong with me. I never thought I deserved more. I do now."

She sucked in a deep breath and put her hand on her stomach, as though it hurt. It probably did. His own pain was certainly real. Physical. Horrible.

"You know, the irony is I learned that from you too. You showed me that I was worth more than I thought. That I was more than my mistakes. More than my parents showed me I was. I'll always be grateful for that. Not for this, though," she said, turning to head back into the bedroom, probably to collect her clothes. "This hurts. And I think you're selling both of us short. I think we could have something, and you're too afraid to take it."

He closed his eyes, ignoring the searing pain in his heart. "No, Maddy. There's nothing. This was nothing."

He'd promised her honesty. Always.

He had broken his promise.

She flinched, her shoulders hunching. But she kept walking, didn't stop. He stood in the middle of the living room, waiting.

When she reemerged she was dressed, her purse slung over her shoulder.

"Will you still be working on the Paris exhibition, or will I need to contract someone else?"

She looked at him, blue eyes hard. "I don't really think it's fair for me to lose my lover and my job on the same day. Plus, I'm good at my job. The best, remember?"

"You'll have your job, any job in my company, as long as you want, Madeline." That he could give her.

She nodded slowly. "Quite the consolation prize. Goodbye, Aleksei."

"Goodbye, Maddy." Her name stuck in his throat, difficult to force it past the lump that had settled there.

She walked past him to the door, where she stopped but didn't turn.

"You know, Aleksei, I finally realized something about myself yesterday. I've been living my life in fear. I let it control what I did, what I didn't do. I let it keep me from so much as going on a date with a man for five years. I don't have room for it anymore. There's no room for fear anymore. Love pushed it away. I hope someday there's a woman who can do the same for you. I know you loved your wife. I know you'll never stop loving her, and I think that's okay. But I hope someday you can let go so that you can move forward."

She opened the door and slipped out into the hallway, shutting the door behind her with a final-sounding click.

Maddy was gone. He'd done what he'd had to.

He waited for the years of hard-won emotionlessness to rescue him from the pain in his body, to rescue him from the dull ache in his head and his heart. From the shattering sensation that was splintering through him.

There was no relief. There was only a sense of bitter loss, a flow of agony that he couldn't stop.

CHAPTER TWELVE

ALEKSEI looked at the bottle of Scotch on his coffee table. He hadn't touched the stuff in five years. Not since the very worst of his grief had passed. Not since he'd realized he wasn't accomplishing anything by drinking his pain away.

He was considering it now. Very seriously.

He couldn't lie to himself and pretend he felt nothing for Maddy, not when the agony of losing her was as acute as it might have been if he'd lost her to death. No, not so bad as that. At least she was still here. At least she had a chance at happiness. With a man who could truly make her happy, give her all she deserved unreservedly.

Although the thought of it made him want to strangle the other man, made rage and pain, so severe it felt beyond his control, pour through him.

Maddy was gone. Sleepless nights were back. He had barely slept at all since she'd walked out of his apartment. Out of his bed and his life.

He reached for the short length of the partially completed necklace that was sitting on the coffee table and ran his fingers over the delicate chain. It had always represented his wife's life to him. Beautiful, but far too short. Incomplete.

Somehow, over the years, it had come to represent his own.

He had continued on. He had made money, found professional success. But his personal life, who he was, had ended.

He'd thought to protect Maddy by sending her away. The simple fact was he'd been protecting himself. Because he was a coward.

He had loved once. Had loved Paulina as a man should love a wife. Losing her had been devastating. It had stripped him of purpose, and he'd had to claw his way out of the pit it had left him in. Find meaning again.

And yet he suspected he hadn't actually found it. He had found stopgaps, things to fill the void temporarily. Bandages that had concealed wounds instead of healing them. But it had been nothing more than vanity. He had more money than one man could spend, more power than most men could exhaust, more fame than he had ever wanted. And yet it was all worthless. Meaningless. He had nothing of value.

He looked at the necklace again and it was Madeline's face he saw.

Maddy, who called up feelings in him he'd thought long buried, who called up feelings deeper than any he'd ever experienced. Maddy, who had his heart.

And if he was going to be the man for her, he had to let go of fear. He had to move on. He tightened his hold on the necklace and pushed the Scotch away.

* * *

Everything was going perfectly at the exhibition. Maddy was standing on the balcony, overlooking the ballroom, watching couples dance to the music.

She smiled wistfully, thinking of the night she'd danced with Aleksei. It seemed like a lifetime ago now. Her memories had a fuzzy edge to them, as though all of it might have been a dream.

If only her pain had the same fuzzy edges as her memories. But it didn't. She missed him so much sometimes she could barely breathe. Over the course of the past week she'd wondered—more than once—if she'd made a mistake.

Being strong and standing on principle, taking all she deserved, was all well and good in theory. It was kind of lonely in reality.

But how could Aleksei—or anyone else—ever respect her if she didn't respect herself? She'd needed to stop letting people who were users dictate the way she saw herself. Dictate the way she saw the entire human race. And she had. She finally had.

It was a hollow victory now, though.

Of course, Aleksei had always respected her. He'd never condemned her for her mistakes. Even in the end he had told her not to accept so little. Not even from him.

It only made her love him more, which just didn't seem fair.

He'd gone back to Moscow the day after. Which was normal. And it was what he'd said he would do. When he was finished in Milan, he wouldn't stay. She'd known then what he'd meant. It was better that he'd done that, really. It made it all feel final. She needed it to feel final so that she could try to accept it and move on.

But, heaven help her, she didn't want to. Loving Aleksei was the most liberating, empowering, terrifying thing she'd ever done. And she didn't want to stop. A good thing, since she wasn't certain she could.

She looked toward the edge of the ballroom and saw Aleksei stride in, looking so amazing in a tailored black suit that she ached with wanting him. He was still so exotic, and yet familiar too. In the very best way. Well, the worst way, really, since she couldn't have him.

He hovered around the edge of the crowd, and she remembered how much he didn't like these kinds of things. She wished she could go down there. Could go and take his hand, ease his tension.

He looked up to the balcony then, his dark eyes zeroing in on her with unerring accuracy. She couldn't do anything but look back, longing and tension stretching between them, thick and obvious, even with so much distance. The physical distance and the emotional distance.

He stepped into the crowd and crossed the dance floor, his focus still on her. She couldn't breathe. She wanted so much to see him again. Just to talk to him, to be near him, if nothing else. And yet she dreaded it too. Dreaded the kind of pain that would come with something like that.

She watched him walk up the curved marble staircase and make his way across the much less empty balcony. She could only stare as he got closer. She didn't know whether to run from him or run to him. The temptation to do both was as intense as it was impossible.

She noticed the difference in his appearance as he drew nearer. He didn't have a tie on. The collar of his shirt was open at his throat. His cheekbones were more prominent, and slight dark circles under his eyes were showing his weariness.

"Maddy." He said so much in that one word, in her name, that it made her heart swell with emotion.

"Hi," she said, hardly able to speak past the lump in her throat.

"Can I speak with you?"

She offered him a small smile. "You're the boss, Mr. Petrov, since when did you start asking permission?"

"Since I realized how fallible my own decision-making was. Please, give me this time."

"Always," she whispered.

He moved to her, took her hand in between both of his and lifted it to his lips, kissing her fingers lightly. When he lowered his hands, she noticed a shiny patch of lighter colored skin.

"What did you do?" she asked, running her thumb over the mark.

"A burn. I was careless with some metal I was working with."

"Aleksei," she said, "you should be more careful."

"I promise I will be." He didn't release his hold on her hand, but walked her to the open double doors that led to an outdoor balcony that overlooked the gardens.

There were fairylights wound around all of the greenery, casting a bright glow on their surroundings. It was late, and it was cold, so the other guests were inside. But Maddy didn't care about the cold. There was nothing but heat when Aleksei was with her.

Aleksei turned so that he was facing the view, his hands gripping the edge of the railing, his burn turning white as he squeezed the stone. "I went back to Moscow to try and escape you. To try and escape my feelings.

I am ashamed to admit this, but you were right. I was afraid. I was living in the past, but not quite in the way you think. I never thought of the rewards that love had given me, only the pain. I was afraid to remember the good things. And then there was you, Maddy. And I wanted you. *You,* not just sex with an anonymous stranger."

She couldn't breathe. Everything in her was wound too tight, her heart pounding too fast.

"And you made me feel," he continued, his voice rough. "I hadn't experienced emotion in so long I hardly recognized it. But I ran from it. I convinced myself I could not be the man for you so I could hide the fact that it was fear that was holding me back."

He reached into the inner pocket of his jacket and pulled out a flat velvet box. "I didn't know if I could be the man for you. But I decided I had to be. Because I can't live without you, Maddy."

He opened the box and Maddy's heart stumbled. "What is this?" she whispered, brushing her fingers over the delicate jewels.

"This." He touched the top of the necklace, by the clasp, the part that was made with intricately woven gold, fashioned into vines with pink gems that resembled small thistle blossoms, the part that looked familiar. "This is my past. I had stopped living, Maddy. I existed, but nothing more. I tricked myself into thinking I had moved on, because I had success, I had money. But it was an illusion."

Maddy felt hot tears burn her eyes, and she let them fall. "What about the rest?" she asked, her voice choked.

The rest of the necklace was made with the same sort of woven gold, but the flowers, fashioned from different-colored gems, grew larger, more open, as they cascaded toward the center. There were emerald leaves, growing, flourishing.

"I had a vision for my life, Maddy, and when that vision changed I simply stopped moving. This…" Aleksei's voice caught and Madeline felt as though her heart might burst. "This isn't how I originally designed this necklace. It's not how I planned my life to be. But it's beautiful, and now…I could not wish it be any other way. My past will always be here." He touched the original part of the necklace. "I will always have love for Paulina. But you have my heart, Maddy. You have reminded me of the beauty of love, have made me open again. You've made me feel. The love I have now…it's endless. Limitless. It's for you. For the family we will have. And it's because of you. I truly understand now what it means to be one with someone. I feel as though you are a part of me. It is unlike anything I've ever known before. I can only hope I have not managed to kill the love you felt for me."

She took a step forward and wrapped her arms around his neck, burying her face in the crook of his neck. She inhaled deeply. Aleksei. Her love.

"No, Aleksei. You haven't killed my love for you. I don't think that's possible."

His chest rose harshly against hers as he sucked in a breath. "Oh, Maddy, you have no idea how happy I am to hear that."

"You are the man that stands before me because of this." She touched the necklace. "I will never ask you to forget."

"I know, Maddy. I can remember now. Remember

and feel some happiness for what was, feel hope for what is to come."

She pulled away from him and he set the velvet case on one of the tables that was set up on the balcony. He carefully lifted the necklace from its place in the box. "I love you, Maddy," he said, holding the necklace up and gently looping the ends around her neck, clasping it deftly. "You are my future, my hope. I love you."

She felt a tear spill down her cheek. Aleksei wiped it away. "Aleksei, you know my past, and you love me anyway. You've helped *me* to love me. And I know, with certainty, that you're my future."

He leaned in and kissed her, and Maddy returned it with all of the joy that was fizzing through her body.

When they separated, Aleksei cupped her chin, his dark eyes serious. "I'm so sorry, Maddy. I promised you honesty, always, and I didn't give it to you. I lied to you. I told you I didn't want you or your love, when even then I wanted both so desperately it destroyed me to send you away. But I had to become a man who was worthy of you. I had to let go—" he touched the center gem of the necklace "—to move on."

"Aleks, you idiot. Don't ever try to protect me by breaking my heart again," she said through a watery laugh.

"It broke mine. I didn't realize that was possible." He bent and kissed her again softly, gently. "I love you, Maddy, more than I thought it was possible to love someone. You are essential to me. I feel as though a piece of myself was missing, and now I'm complete."

"Wow, you don't go halfway, do you?"

"Never." He stroked her cheek. "Thank you for making my future more beautiful than I imagined possible."

"I have to thank you for the same thing," she said softly.

"So, you like the necklace?" he asked.

"Of course I do."

"If you want it." He reached into his pocket and produced another velvet box, this one smaller. "I have a matching piece."

"Aleks…"

He opened it and revealed a ring with colorful gemstones encircling an emerald-cut diamond, tiny platinum vines carved into the band. "If you'll marry me, then it was worth the burn that I got making it."

"Yes," she whispered as she held out her shaking hand. He slipped it onto her finger. A perfect fit, in every way.

"When I said future, I meant future. Every day of it. There are no guarantees in life, Maddy, but one thing I can promise is that you have my love."

"Then I don't need any other guarantees."

EPILOGUE

"Do you know how happy it makes me to see you like this? With a smile on your face?"

Maddy looked up at her older brother and squeezed his arm. "Thank you, Gage. It means a lot to me that you came to give me away."

"I wouldn't miss it."

"You really took care of me when no one else would. I don't know if I've ever told you how much that meant to me."

Gage looked at her. "It was never a sacrifice, Maddy. I would do it again in a heartbeat. I love you."

"I love you too."

Maddy smiled and craned her neck to see if she could spot Aleksei down the hill. The wedding was being held outside of the castle in Luxembourg. And tonight they were having their honeymoon in that princess suite Maddy had been so fond of.

The trees had white and red paper lanterns in them, and each chair was draped in white chiffon, the covers tied on with red bows. It was all exquisitely beautiful, and perfect. The wedding of her dreams.

The setting didn't really matter, though. The only

thing that really mattered was the groom, and how much she loved him.

The first song ended and Maddy knew the "Wedding March" was about to begin. Butterflies swirled in her belly. Not nerves, just pure, unreserved excitement.

She smoothed the full skirt of her wedding gown and gripped her bouquet of red roses tightly.

"Ready?" Gage asked.

"More than," Maddy said.

As she walked down the green hill and to the aisle, Aleksei came into view. He smiled when he saw her, his dark eyes glittering.

In Aleks's eyes she saw her future. A life stretched before them filled with endless possibilities. A family. Children. Love. So much love that she couldn't contain all of it inside of herself. It was her own fairytale, come to life and more brilliant than anything she could have ever dreamed up on her own.

They had conquered so much darkness, overcome so much to reach this moment. With all of that behind them, there was nothing that could defeat them. Not when they were bound together by so much love.

Aleksei shook Gage's hand when they reached the head of the aisle. Then it was just her and Aleksei.

He took her hand and pressed his lips to her knuckles. "You're beautiful," he said.

And she believed him.

* * * * *

CLASSIC

Quintessential, modern love stories
that are romance at its finest.

COMING NEXT MONTH from Harlequin Presents® EXTRA
AVAILABLE FEBRUARY 14, 2012

#185 ONE DESERT NIGHT
One Night In...
Maggie Cox

**#186 ONE NIGHT IN THE
ORIENT**
One Night In...
Robyn Donald

**#187 INTERVIEW WITH
THE DAREDEVIL**
Unbuttoned by a Rebel
Nicola Marsh

**#188 SECRET HISTORY OF
A GOOD GIRL**
Unbuttoned by a Rebel
Aimee Carson

COMING NEXT MONTH from Harlequin Presents®
AVAILABLE FEBRUARY 28, 2012

**#3047 A SHAMEFUL
CONSEQUENCE**
The Secrets of Xanos
Carol Marinelli

**#3048 AN OFFER SHE CAN'T
REFUSE**
Emma Darcy

**#3049 THE END OF HER
INNOCENCE**
Sara Craven

**#3050 THE THORN IN
HIS SIDE**
21st Century Bosses
Kim Lawrence

**#3051 STRANGERS IN
THE DESERT**
Lynn Raye Harris

**#3052 FORBIDDEN TO
HIS TOUCH**
Natasha Tate

You can find more information on upcoming Harlequin® titles,
free excerpts and more at www.HarlequinInsideRomance.com.

HPCNM0212

REQUEST YOUR
FREE BOOKS!

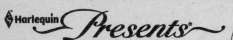 

2 FREE NOVELS PLUS
2 FREE GIFTS!

YES! Please send me 2 FREE Harlequin Presents® novels and my 2 FREE gifts (gifts are worth about $10). After receiving them, if I don't wish to receive any more books, I can return the shipping statement marked "cancel." If I don't cancel, I will receive 6 brand-new novels every month and be billed just $4.30 per book in the U.S. or $4.99 per book in Canada. That's a saving of at least 14% off the cover price! It's quite a bargain! Shipping and handling is just 50¢ per book in the U.S. and 75¢ per book in Canada.* I understand that accepting the 2 free books and gifts places me under no obligation to buy anything. I can always return a shipment and cancel at any time. Even if I never buy another book, the two free books and gifts are mine to keep forever.

106/306 HDN FERQ

Name _____ (PLEASE PRINT) _____

Address _____ Apt. # _____

City _____ State/Prov. _____ Zip/Postal Code _____

Signature (if under 18, a parent or guardian must sign) _____

Mail to the **Reader Service:**
IN U.S.A.: P.O. Box 1867, Buffalo, NY 14240-1867
IN CANADA: P.O. Box 609, Fort Erie, Ontario L2A 5X3

Not valid for current subscribers to Harlequin Presents books.

**Are you a current subscriber to Harlequin Presents books
and want to receive the larger-print edition?
Call 1-800-873-8635 or visit www.ReaderService.com.**

* Terms and prices subject to change without notice. Prices do not include applicable taxes. Sales tax applicable in N.Y. Canadian residents will be charged applicable taxes. Offer not valid in Quebec. This offer is limited to one order per household. All orders subject to credit approval. Credit or debit balances in a customer's account(s) may be offset by any other outstanding balance owed by or to the customer. Please allow 4 to 6 weeks for delivery. Offer available while quantities last.

Your Privacy—The Reader Service is committed to protecting your privacy. Our Privacy Policy is available online at www.ReaderService.com or upon request from the Reader Service.

We make a portion of our mailing list available to reputable third parties that offer products we believe may interest you. If you prefer that we not exchange your name with third parties, or if you wish to clarify or modify your communication preferences, please visit us at www.ReaderService.com/consumerschoice or write to us at Reader Service Preference Service, P.O. Box 9062, Buffalo, NY 14269. Include your complete name and address.

HPI1B

New York Times *and* USA TODAY *bestselling author Maya Banks presents book three in her miniseries* PREGNANCY & PASSION.

TEMPTED BY HER INNOCENT KISS

Available March 2012 from Harlequin Desire!

There came a time in a man's life when he knew he was well and truly caught. Devon Carter stared down at the diamond ring nestled in velvet and acknowledged that this was one such time. He snapped the lid closed and shoved the box into the breast pocket of his suit.

He had two choices. He could marry Ashley Copeland and fulfill his goal of merging his company with Copeland Hotels, thus creating the largest, most exclusive line of resorts in the world, or he could refuse and lose it all.

Put in that light, there wasn't much he could do except pop the question.

The doorman to his Manhattan high-rise apartment hurried to open the door as Devon strode toward the street. He took a deep breath before ducking into his car, and the driver pulled into traffic.

Tonight was the night. All of his careful wooing, the countless dinners, kisses that started brief and casual and became more breathless—all a lead-up to tonight. Tonight his seduction of Ashley Copeland would be complete, and then he'd ask her to marry him.

He shook his head as the absurdity of the situation hit him for the hundredth time. Personally, he thought William Copeland was crazy for forcing his daughter down Devon's throat.

Ashley was a sweet enough girl, but Devon had no desire

to marry anyone.

William had other plans. He'd told Devon that Ashley had no head for the family business. She was too softhearted, too naive. So he'd made Ashley part of the deal. The catch? Ashley wasn't to know of it. Which meant Devon was stuck playing stupid games.

Ashley was supposed to think this was a grand love match. She was a starry-eyed woman who preferred her animal-rescue foundation over board meetings, charts and financials for Copeland Hotels.

If she ever found out the truth, she wouldn't take it well.

And hell, he couldn't blame her.

But no matter the reason for his proposal, before the night was over, she'd have no doubts that she belonged to him.

What will happen when Devon marries Ashley?
Find out in Maya Banks's passionate new novel
TEMPTED BY HER INNOCENT KISS
Available March 2012 from Harlequin Desire!